ALL FOR THE LOVE ~~OF A LADY~~—
"A SUPER-DUPER"

". . . a splendid blend of love and murder in Washington. Narrated with abundant charm and excitement . . . This will keep you wide-eyed and goggling"

—BOOKS

"Neatly put together"

—THE NEW YORKER

"Very pleasant murder"

—WASHINGTON STAR

LESLIE FORD

ALL FOR THE LOVE OF A LADY

WILDSIDE PRESS

All for the Love of a Lady

Published by Wildside Press LLC
wildsidepress.com | bcmystery.com

1

If you've ever lived in Washington in the summer, you know what a jar of Victory garden tomatoes feels like in a pressure cooker. The pressure would be bad enough at any time, of course, but it's easier to take when there's snow on Capitol Hill, and when stewing in one's own juice is a figurative expression, applied to public heads about to roll back to private life.

The fact that it was July and not January may have had no effect on the end of the Crane-Durbin business, but it had plenty on the beginning. If Molly Crane had been busy thawing out the drain-pipes of their small house in Georgetown, and Courtney Durbin had spent her time at the telephone, as she swore she did, trying to get an extra teacupful of oil from the ration board to heat their large house on Massachusetts Avenue, neither of them would have been at the Abbotts' pool on that Wednesday night. Of course, better men than I—especially since I'm Grace Latham and a woman . . . widow, actually, on what a kind friend once said was the glamorous side of forty—better men than I have said that "if" is the most bootless word in any language. It's only a point on the circumference of a vicious circle, or at best the starting place of an endless chain stretching nowhere. If Courtney Durbin had married Cass Crane, as everybody expected her to for years, she wouldn't have married that singular but very rich newcomer to Washington with the war, Mr. D. J. Durbin. If she'd married Cass, Cass wouldn't have married Molly. And Molly might have married Randy Fleming, who'd always adored her. And it would have saved a lot of trouble.

Whether Colonel Primrose and his indomitable Sergeant Buck, those partners in experting crime who prowl about the ambiguous periphery where the Intelligence agencies in Washington tend to coordinate, would have been drawn, or wouldn't have been drawn, into a murder hunt by eight o'clock the next morning, is hard to say. When one part of a pattern is gone, who can tell that any other part of it would ever have existed? Or perhaps the incident at the Abbotts' pool was itself only part of a pattern already formed, or a chain of circumstances already grimly in motion.

So if nobody at all had been at the Abbotts' that night it might not have saved any blood . . . though that's figurative too, for through the whole affair no bright red drop was ever visible, unless on the moon that night. But it would have saved something else.

5

Furthermore, if enough people know you'd like to commit murder, it might get pretty hard to convince all of them you didn't. You could never again be sure, meeting a quietly scrutinizing eye before it was turned away, across a table or a room, that that wasn't the thought behind it. The people who think Duleep Singh is clairvoyant, and there are a lot of them, said it was behind his when he said, "There is blood on that moon."

He said it to me, because I was sitting next to him on the rim of the Abbotts' pink marble fountain basin, but it was in one of those moments when everybody suddenly and inexplicably stops talking, and it reached everywhere, against a background of softly, eerily dripping water. Charlie, the Abbotts' loathsome pet bullfrog, croaked hoarsely from under a lily pad, and when Corinne Blodgett said, "Duleep Singh says there's blood on the moon," her voice was more like Charlie's than Singh's.

"Whose blood, I wonder?"

Courtney Durbin's voice was cool and soft like the dripping water.

"—Can you tell us, Mr. Singh?"

"You should know, Mrs. Durbin."

Corinne Blodgett said he emphasized the "you" ever so slightly, but I didn't hear it that way.

"—Aren't men killing each other all over the world, tonight?"

Corinne said he just added that, with a perceptible pause in between, and also that his dark eyes were fixed significantly on Courtney. But Corinne lived a year on dates, nuts and goat's milk and cheese, and wore sandals only when the chauffeur refused to take her driving with nothing on but a coarse linen robe. Corinne's an awful fool, in some ways, but a really sweet one, and probably makes more sense in the long run than most women do.

Molly Crane was sitting in one of those elaborate terrace chaise longues with the rubber-tired wheels at the back. Or she had been up to that moment, with Randy Fleming perched on the end of the chaise, his new wings on his shirt, one hand playing with the gay red butterfly bow on her slipper beside him. Just then she wasn't sitting. At the sound of Courtney Durbin's voice her body went taut as a bowstring, and her hand holding a long glass of iced lemonade moved slowly out to put it down on the low table at her elbow. Her face in the dusk was a pointed white blur turned toward Courtney, with two spots of liquid flame where her eyes were. The blur was a charged magnetic fluid, and even Duleep Singh's voice, suavely Oriental in spite of its Oxford accent, seemed to crackle a little as it crossed it. One foot moved from the other. She was like a cat getting ready to spring,

6

and Courtney Durbin knew it, as did everyone else sitting there. There wasn't only blood on the moon just then. It was in Molly's eyes, and in Courtney's, and in Randy Fleming's, I think. His hand clamped down on Molly's ankle, pinning it to the yellow leather cushion so sharply that her body quivered for an instant.

She relaxed slowly and raised her glass to her lips again. We all relaxed, politely and unobtrusively, trying not to seem to do so, and Randy took his hand off her ankle. Courtney Durbin dropped her cigarette on the terrace and rubbed it dead with the toe of her shoe. She reached over to the ivory box on the table for another.

"You must be frightfully excited about Cass coming home, Molly," she said deliberately, glancing at Randy Fleming across the spurt of flame Duleep Singh held to the tip of her cigarette.

Molly sat up abruptly, not like a cat now but like a flash of lightning.

"Cass—coming . . . ?"

Then she gasped. It was a tiny, barely audible sound as she realized, I suppose, that she'd stepped like a day-old lamb into a trap that was yawning for her. But it was too late.

Courtney Durbin gasped too, but it was very different.

"Oh, I'm sorry! Maybe it's a military secret . . . but, darling, I thought if he sent me word, he'd certainly . . . Oh, I'm frightfully sorry! But after all, he's your husband, isn't he? How should I——"

Randy Fleming's hand closed over Molly's ankle again.

"He's sent you word, all right, if he is coming," he said, in a kind of determined drawl. "It's just got tangled up in red tape . . ."

"Oh, of course, darling," Courtney said. She got up. "I must go. I hate to, it's such fun here."

She looked around at Duleep Singh. "—Can I take anybody any place on my way? This is a business trip—I just stopped in on my way to the airport."

She hesitated an instant. "Cass wanted somebody to meet him. Would you like to come and surprise him, Molly?"

Molly Crane was staring ahead of her, past Randy Fleming, at the big red globe of the rising moon. She started a little and turned her head.

"No, thanks," she said. "Just tell him to be careful. I painted the bathroom this morning, and it probably isn't dry yet."

Randy Fleming got up abruptly.

"Let's go, Molly. It won't be a surprise. He's expecting you all right."

He held out his hand to hoist her up.

She didn't move or put out her hand.

"I'm staying here, thanks."

He stood there helplessly for a moment, and sat down at her feet again. It's where he'd been—practically, I thought— since they were children, except the day she married Cass Crane, less than five months before. He spent that day at various places, which I've been assured is one of the reasons the per capita consumption of hard liquor will be higher in Washington than anywhere else in the country this year.

In the silence that followed Courtney's departure a woman, obviously from the very deep South, said, "Is there a Mr. Durbin?"

There was another silence at that. Whether it was because she hadn't asked anyone in particular, or whether she was so evidently an outsider, in not knowing that there was indeed a Mr. Durbin, that the pack closed defensively in, I don't know. Nobody said anything, and it was just as well, for at that moment the screen door in the middle of the long pillared verandah across the back of the house opened. It was the first time I, for one, had ever seen D. J. Durbin at any private house except Courtney's before she married him, the first autumn of the War, and his own since.

He stood silhouetted against the lighted porch for an instant, a slight almost grotesque figure, leaning on his stick, one shoulder plainly lower than the other in spite of his built-up shoe. I could see him clearly in the dusk, because he'd been sharply etched on my mind from the first day I met him . . . his twisted foot and hippity-hoppity gait, his saffron-yellow complexion and aquiline nose, and the dark hair frosted with gray. His eyes should be icy-gray too, but they're fine and dark, and his lips full instead of being thin and like a steel trap. Because of that it's hard to say what made his face the most ruthless one I'd ever seen, but it was. It doesn't seem to me we used to have people like him around, before the War brought its cross-section of the strange international world to the sprawling city that used to sleep all summer by the Potomac. Or if they came here, they stayed in smoke-filled hotel rooms, and left as quickly as they could, bored with a provincial and isolated puritanism. They may still be bored, now, but they have to stay here, in the new center of the world.

I glanced at Duleep Singh, wondering if the moon and the sound of playing water made his inner ear listen for silver bells on the feet of dancing girls. Apparently not, I thought. The rose-colored light under the fountain spray threw his dark handsome face into a deeper shadow, but the rising moon-glow touched it as it might a bronze Buddha in a shadowy shrine. His gaze was fixed on Molly Crane. It was sombre and profoundly brooding. The contrast between them was so extraordinary that for a moment it was alarming. There's an experiment they do in the psychology laboratories in a sound-proof chamber. where the noise of people's pumping hearts slowly becomes audible, deafening, terrifying. In a way that was what was happening with Molly Crane just then. Without an apparent motion there was such a turmoil of revolt and hurt pride there, anger and unhappiness, that she was like a centrifugal churn. And it was only against Duleep Singh's field of hypnotic calm that it could have showed. There was something extraordinary about it. Up to then I'd thought the women who said, from the day he arrived in Washington on some kind of mission from New Delhi, "My dear, isn't he *fascinating!*" were a little silly. But as the moonlight glistened now on the startling whites of his eyes I found myself moving uneasily, and wanting Randy Fleming, or Cass Crane, or somebody, to take Molly away from there. She was too young and too transparent. It wasn't fair, because within the limits of her own small orbit she was covering up very well. So well, in fact, that Corinne Blodgett, who thinks herself psychic, said later, "If Molly had *really* cared, my dear. she wouldn't have just *sat* there."

Then the spell broke. Duleep Singh turned his head, got up and bowed as Courtney's husband came around the pink marble fountain basin to where we were sitting. I was sorry the spell had gone . . . I would have liked to see D. J. Durbin as taansparently revealed as Molly Crane had been.

He stopped and spoke abruptly, barely nodding to any of us.

"Has Mrs. Durbin gone?"

"About five minutes ago."

It was Randy who answered. And it may have been the pack rallying again. Nobody, not even Molly, said where she'd gone, or that she'd gone to meet Cass Crane. And he couldn't not know about Cass, not possibly. Even if he'd been deaf as a post he must have heard the gasp that went up when Courtney married him and not Cass. And if he hadn't heard what Courtney said when Cass suddenly and astonishingly married Molly—and what she was still saying—then he was the only person within a hundred miles who hadn't. Or perhaps, of course, he didn't care. He simply turned on his heel, now, and went limping back to the house and out of sight, without saying good night or thank you.

I glanced at Molly. She was looking up at the sky, waiting for Cass's plane to fly across, I suppose, her small face as pale and empty and inscrutable, now, as the moon-washed bowl above her.

The marble basin rim I was sitting on seemed to get hard and uncomfortable. It wasn't any hotter than it had been all

9

evening, but the atmosphere had gone stale, like flat luke-warm champagne. It was dull and oppressive, and something it just seemed better to be out of.

"I think I'll go home," I said.

Duleep Singh smiled and bowed. "May I——"

I shook my head. "No, thanks. I'm taking the bus, and it stops at my door. Good night."

I didn't go across to the other side of the garden to say goodbye to my host, who was talking to Corinne Blodgett's husband Horace and some other men in a secluded corner. It's one of the rules of the house that guests go as they please, without making other people feel it must be getting late. As I stopped at the dressing room at the end of the porch to get my umbrella—wishful thinking of the school that doesn't believe it's bound to rain if you *don't* take it—I heard the Southern lady checking up again.

"Now, who was that, dear?"

"That's Grace Latham."

It was Corinne Blodgett answering, and the next question was obvious.

"No, dear, he's dead. She just lives here because it happens to be her home. She's one of us odd people who were *born* here."

Even if I could have heard the rest of it I wouldn't have had to bother. It's like a record that goes on automatically once the needle's in place.—No, she's never married again, and nobody knows why. She has two sons, but they're no excuse because one's an air cadet and the other's away at school. She certainly could have, if for no other reason than because she's got a house in Georgetown. Just a hall bedroom will get a woman a husband in Washington these days. Yes, she does have men around. Especially Colonel Primrose. Some people say he wants to marry her, but either she won't or he doesn't or that granite Sergeant he lives with won't let him. And so on . . .

I feel sorry for Colonel John Primrose, 92nd Engineers U.S.A. (Retired), sometimes. If ever a man is forced to turn over his ration books to prove publicly that his intentions are not dishonorable, or that he is not a worm under the heel of a Sergeant Phineas T. Buck, also 92nd Engineers, U.S.A., also retired, it will be Colonel Primrose. There really ought to be a Fifth Freedom—For Men Only. Though frankly it's got to the point where I almost wish he really would ask me to marry him, so I could settle it for everybody . . . one way or the other.

2

I went out through the rose-and-white marble-paved hall, bare of rugs for the summer, and down to the street. In ordinary times the narrow road leading out to Connecticut Avenue would have been lined with cars. There were only two there now. One had a diplomatic marker, and the other was a long sleek black job with a tiny troglodyte of a man leaning against the fender, fanning himself with a panama hat. I looked around, because it was like seeing a shadow without its substance. Then I saw the substance. He was standing by the luminous white board with diagonal black stripes that marks the dead end of the road where it falls sharply off down into the Park. He was leaning on his stick, looking up into the sky . . . as intently, it seemed to me, as Molly Crane had done.

As I got almost to the sidewalk, Achille, the little dwarf of a chauffeur, opened the door of the big car and turned on the lights. D. J. Durbin still stood there for a moment as though listening, then started toward the car, the dull *thub* of his rubber-capped stick punctuating the drag of his lame foot and the staccato clack of his good one on the cobblestones. And suddenly the most weird and extraordinary sound came out of the little creature by the car. I drew back as instinctively as if I'd heard a rattlesnake warning me from the grass. But the warning was not for me. Mr. Durbin halted abruptly, fell back a step and flung up his stick, beating the air wildly with it. Achille leaped forward across the walk. A black cat, blinded by the sudden glare of the headlights, was in the act of jumping off the wall to cross the road. Faced with the thrashing stick and the driver's waving arms, it turned tail and lit back up through the shrubbery the way it had come.

D. J. Durbin leaned heavily on his stick, pulled out a handkerchief and mopped his forehead, and I stood gaping at both of them until I caught myself and hurried on up the street. The motor whirred then, and the car shot past me over the hump toward Connecticut Avenue as if the devil were still after it. Then, as it disappeared, in the empty stillness of the street I heard the heavy drone of a plane overhead. It was still high, its red light looking like an outlaw star, disembodied as if the plane itself had dissolved against the luminous backdrop of the vacant sky.

I know spotters who can tell what a plane is by the sound of its motor, or say they can. Perhaps it's true, because Sheila, my Irish setter, never disturbs herself, lying in the hall half

11

asleep, for any car but mine pulling up at the curb. Whether D. J. Durbin or Achille knew what plane that was, before the business of the black cat, I don't know. It may have had nothing to do with their abrupt departure at all. It certainly had something to do with Molly's.

I heard her heels clicking up the walk behind me and her voice calling my name. She was running up the narrow pavement, turning from silver into gold as she came out of the phosphorescent moonglow into the murky yellow cone under the old street lamp, and to silver again as she came through it. Randy was pounding along behind her. It seemed to me that all I could see for an instant as she stopped was a couple of hot liquid blobs in her face where people normally have eyes. There were tears in them, and she was batting them back, trying not to let us see them. But in that pale light tears glisten, even when a face is indistinct.

"Grace," she said abruptly, "—have you got company?"

I shook my head a little blankly. "Why?"

"Then would you let me stay all night tonight?"

"Now wait a minute, Molly!"

I didn't have to look at Randy's African sun-scorched face under the thatch of burnt-up hair that used to be brown to see that he was taking the whole business as hard as Molly was. His voice was enough.

"I'm not staying in that house tonight," Molly said quietly. "I said I wouldn't, and I'm not. If Grace won't let me stay with her I'll . . . I'll go to a hotel."

"They're all full," Randy said. "Don't be a dope. Give the guy a break, won't you? He'd have let you know if he could have."

"He let Courtney know, didn't he? If he could get word to her, he could to me—if he'd wanted to."

"Maybe she just heard it tonight. If you'd been home you——"

She shook her head. "Courtney's known it the last four days. I knew there was something, the way she's been acting. I've been wondering what it was.—And don't tell me I'm crazy. I've had just all I can take."

Her voice quivered a little.

"Can I stay with you, Grace?"

"Of course," I said.

Randy shrugged. "No use standing here till we draw a crowd. I'll get a taxi. You can do as you please."

He strode on toward Connecticut Avenue, and I started on as Molly stood there for an instant fishing around in her bag for her compact.

It was hard to know what to do. If she'd been married to anybody but Cass Crane, if he'd let anybody but Courtney Durbin know he was coming back, it might have been

12

easier. Any other man coming home to a girl he'd married and left a week afterwards, to be gone four or five months heaven knows where, would have deserved every benefit of the doubt. But somehow not Cass. It may all just have gone back to the fact that Cass was the man every gal who'd come out in Washington for the last five years had decided she wanted to marry. But he'd belonged to Courtney, and nobody could get him away. When she married D. J. Durbin and it was assumed he was on the block again, the postman literally staggered up his front steps. But he was at the Durbins' just as he'd been at Courtney's own house before, and he and Courtney were at all the same parties together, because D. J. Durbin didn't go out and Cass went in his place. Then he was sent to South America, and came home one Thursday. He and Molly were married on Saturday, and he was gone the next Saturday. And now . . .

She'd caught up with me on the narrow sidewalk.

"—Do you suppose he's forgotten he married me?"

"I . . . think he'd remember, darling," I said. "At least, it's customary."

"I mean, seriously. He might have got a fever, or . . . something. I mean . . . well, I haven't heard from him for a long time, and Courtney told somebody he wouldn't have married me if he'd——"

"You mean he had a fever when he married you," I said. "And now he's over it, and he's forgotten, the way you'd forget a delirium?"

She didn't say anything for a moment.

"I know it doesn't make any sense. Anyway, I don't want to stay at home tonight, Grace."

There was a catch in her voice again.

"I'd just make a scene . . . or I'd act as if it didn't matter. And—it's got to be either me or Courtney. It can't be both. It just won't work that way. I'm not that . . . that smart."

"All right, Molly," I said. We were at the top of the slope and Randy was waiting on the corner with a taxi. "You come to my house tonight, and tomorrow you can see."

It wasn't to be quite that simple.

"I guess I ought to stop by the house a minute," she said when we got in the cab. "I . . . I've got to get a toothbrush, and my uniform."

"Right," Randy said. He told the driver. His voice was casual and matter-of-fact, but he took hold of her hand and gave it a tight squeeze. If he hadn't been in love with her, I suppose, he wouldn't have been standing by as he was, though it's always seemed to me the young are capable of a lot more unselfishness than they're given credit for. If an occasional eyebrow had been raised about these two, it would have reflected more on the minds of the raisers than on them. And Courtney's calling Molly a whited sepulchre, and a two-timing little rat, has always seemed to me rather ironic to say the least. The trouble with Courtney is the trouble with a lot of women whose mothers forgot to tell them about eating their cake and having it too, and making their bed and lying in it, and those other useful bits of information preserved in the domestic time-capsules of yester-year. Though at the moment and on the face of it, Courtney Durbin seemed positive proof that such things are as obsolete as the recipe for A Very Nice Face Pomade made out of mutton tallow and attar of roses that I've still got at home, in my great-grandmother's spidery script.

The taxi slowed down on 26th, and turned a little dubiously, as well it might, into the end of Beall Street. Molly and Cass's house is the only one in the block that has so far reversed the blight that most of the rest of Georgetown has been rescued from, to become a landlord's Garden of Eden with the Rent Control Board its only serpent . . . if an anaemic gartersnake can so be called. It's the second house from the corner. They bought it the day they were married, from a cousin of my cook Lilac who'd got a war job and was moving to civilized quarters. It looked then as if it would collapse in an unlovely heap of rotten boards if you bounced a ping-pong ball off it. The house next door on the corner, by the parked space above the drive along Rock Creek, was both too expensive and too far gone . . . so far gone, in fact, that it's still empty, rats and fungi its only life, an old wisteria vine and the boards nailed across the sashless windows all that holds it together at all. The house we stopped at had no resemblance whatever to its original self or to any of its neighbors. It was gleaming white, with green shutters and window boxes full of hanging begonias.

On the uneven brick sidewalk Molly stopped short and listened intently.

"—Isn't that my phone?"

She ran through the white gate and up the iron steps. I could hear the muffled peal of the bell sounding again. She got the key out of her bag, unlocked the door and ran in.

"She's done a swell job, hasn't she?" Randy said casually. He looked up at the white face of the little house. "She damn near killed herself, scraping and painting and patching plaster.—God, I hope that's him, the stinking . . ."

He stopped without finishing it. We stood there listening. We could have heard her voice, but we didn't, and then a light went on in the back room, making a yellow path through the doorway. We went up the steps and inside.

Molly was in the front room, staring down into the fire-

14

place. As Randy switched on the light she turned around and smiled, quickly and too brightly.

"They'd hung up."

"Then let's stick around till he calls again." Randy said. "He probably didn't even know you were living here. He wouldn't have had a key——"

She put her hand on his arm.

"You're sweet, Randy—but . . . don't! Please don't!" She tried to smile. "I'll get my things. If you want a drink there's some ice downstairs."

She went out into the tiny hallway and up the stairs. I could hear her feet going across the floor and the creak of a bed, and that was all.

Randy stood there a moment, pulling a brush hair out of a blob of paint on the mantel.

"I'll get some ice," he said curtly. "God, this makes me sore. A guy like that . . ."

"Listen," I said patiently. "There *must* have been a slip-up. I can't *believe* there wasn't."

The look he gave me made me feel old and infirm and feebleminded.

"—I was going to get some ice, wasn't I."

I waited. It was the first time I'd been in the house since she'd painted the woodwork. If you looked too carefully the old chocolate-brown still showed in places, but it was very pleasant, and a superhuman job in this weather. And now she was upstairs alone with it, and all the fun it was going to be to show Cass what she could do, in between being a nurse's aide four hours a day and working at the ration board and all the other things she did, was lying like a lump of uncooked dough in the pit of her stomach.

Downstairs I could hear Randy swearing at the ice cubes. From outside in the street came a burst of high laughter from some unrestrained libido, full rich voices from the colored church around the corner drowning it suddenly with "Marching Down the King's Highway." In the warm duskiness of the surrounding night the little house with its smell of wet plaster and fresh paint seemed very pathetic and young and lonely.

I could hear Randy plodding up the stairs, ice clinking against glass, and the creak of the floor above as Molly began to move around again. Suddenly the phone rang in the back room. Randy stopped, ice bucket in hand, looking at it, his lean sunburned face expressionless. The next instant Molly was flying downstairs. She'd changed her dress and taken off her evening slippers. She was barefooted, with one shoe in her hand, her face lighted up in a poignantly transparent denial of everything she'd said before.

15

When she said "Hello," her voice was a further betrayal, and it was even more of one when she said, "Oh, hello, Courtney."

She listened silently for a moment.

"Thanks a lot for calling. No, I'm sorry, darling, but I've got to be at the hospital at the crack of dawn. I'll see him tomorrow. Goodbye."

When she turned her face was drained of everything. Even her eyes were pale. She shook her head and picked up her shoe from the table by the phone.

"Cass is at the Durbins'," she said calmly. "He was too busy to come to the phone. Courtney wanted me to come over."

She went back to the hall. "I'll be down in a second, Grace. Will you see the lights are off downstairs, please, Randy?"

She'd just got upstairs when a woman's voice called from the street—"Yoo-hoo, Molly! Cass?"—and we heard a lot of feet scraping up the iron steps.

3

I recognized Julie Ross's voice.

"Hello, angels, can we come in a minute? We didn't know you'd got home till we saw you through the kitch——"

Julie came in through the front room door and stopped short, her face blank for an instant.

"Oh, hello, Grace. Hello, Randy. We thought it was Cass and Molly."

The "we" consisted, besides herself, of one large, fat-faced untidy man with a lot of moist black hair, his pongee suit dripping wet, and a man with a long face, gray hair and a quick pair of slate-blue eyes who looked as if he'd stopped on the top step, taken a cool shower and stepped into a linen suit just off the ironing board. He looked, furthermore, as acutely embarrassed as he was cool. The large man did neither. He was very hot and not embarrassed in the least. He was almost a comic strip figure, I thought, he had such a waggish good humor about him. It wasn't until I looked beyond the smile-crinkled bags around his eyes that I had the slightly uncomfortable feeling that if I had to meet one of them on a dark night, the other one would be safer.

Julie waved her hand toward them without looking around.

"—Do you know these people?"

"No," Randy said. He added, "Do you? And who are they?"

"Don't pay any attention to him, anybody," Julie said. "The clean one's Mr. Austin, and I can't pronounce the other one's name so it doesn't matter. Anyway, it was Cass we wanted to see. Somebody said he was getting back tonight. I thought maybe he'd run into my sainted husband out in the wilds, and I thought I'd like to know whether he's still alive or can I start looking around. I don't suppose you'd like to give us a drink."

"Have a cigarette," Randy said. He pulled a moist unattractive pack out of his pocket. "Grace and I just decided alcohol makes you hotter and the hell with it. If you'll just stick around a few minutes you can have the whole place to yourselves. We're shoving off."

"Oh, I see," Julie said brightly. "You want us to stay. Sweetie, I'm sorry, but we've got to go. Fresh paint makes us break out. Tell Molly goodbye. Goodbye, Grace."

The two gentlemen backed out, the immaculate Mr. Austin bowing politely and still more embarrassed, the large wet man with the unpronounceable name looking hotter and wetter and still more good-humored.

"Goodbye, Randy dear," Julie called back. "If you ever have to make a crash landing I hope it's in a nice field of poison ivy."

I heard them close the gate. Randy stood looking at me.

"Now, how the hell did they know Cass was due in?" he asked grimly. "I know that big wet guy. Wait a minute—he signed my short snorter bill in Cairo a couple of years ago."

He pulled out his wallet and held a tattered dollar bill under the light on the table.

"Here we are," he said. " 'Lons Sondauer.' "

He looked at me again. "Where the devil could Julie have picked him up? He's some kind of great big screwball—rich as a skunk."

"Did he recognize you?"

He shook his head. "I don't think so, I wasn't in uniform then.—I'd like to know what this is all about, Grace. Julie isn't turning an honest penny introducing the right people, is she?"

He grinned at me suddenly. "You may have gathered that Mrs. Ross gives me a pain."

Molly was just coming down.

"Half a second," she said. She went to the little panelled cupboard set in the wall in the back room and took out a bottle of Scotch. "I'd just like to . . . welcome the prodigal —if he happens to come back."

She smiled quickly at us and went out into the hall and down to the dining room. In a minute she came back with a Waterford decanter with the usual silver chain and plaque around its neck. She put it down on the cocktail bar impro-

17

vised from an old-fashioned washstand, and set Randy's thermos tub beside it.

"There," she said. "Let's go before somebody else drops in."

She looked at Randy for an instant. "You shouldn't have been rude to Julie Ross. She hasn't heard from Spud for months, and his family have practically told her they'll take the kids and she can support herself. That's one thing about Courtney, even if I do have to say it. Julie'd just about have been in the street if it hadn't been for her."

"She can afford it," Randy said calmly.

"So can a lot of people, but they don't."

Molly closed my front door behind Randy and came back into the sitting room. It used to open out onto a green lawn with masses of flowers in the borders against the brick wall. Now it opens onto something that has very little resemblance to the idea I had when calluses meant nothing, and I had a vision of a horn of plenty, with young carrots and stringless tender beans and tiny yellow squash rolling out of it onto my dinner table, with possibly a dewy basketful for the Old Ladies' Home. That was when I was reading the front of the seed catalogue, and hadn't bothered to look in the back, at the pictures of sprays and the price of rotenone and nicotine and copper sulphate, or even remotely suspected the infinity of various-legged things that make a leaf without holes chewed in it an unbelievable miracle. Still, the pungent smell of a ripe unpicked tomato has something that ambergris and all the perfumes of Arabia don't have. I was sniffing it through the open window, hoping that the night's invisible invasion would leave a few of them intact for the morning—not round and rosy like in the pictures but deformed and misshapen, poor things but mine own—when I heard Molly cross the room behind me.

I looked around. She'd gone over to the fireplace and was sitting in the wing chair, staring at some point a long ways past the blackened bricks in front of her, paying no attention to Sheila's paw resting on her knee.

I haven't said very much about what Molly Crane looks like, because it's a little hard to say. It depends so much on what's going on inside her. If she and Courtney Durbin were sitting side by side—which was beginning to appear increasingly unlikely—hardly anyone would look twice at her, because Courtney is a really beautiful woman. But if one did look twice, with a perceptive eye, he'd see there was something there. It's an intangible quality, difficult to name. There's not more than four years' difference between her age and Courtney's—twenty-two, and twenty-six or so—but in the terms other than years that make people seem younger

18

or older there's more difference than that. I suppose it's the difference between having a gardener in to plant your radishes and doing it yourself, or having the maid walk the dog on a leash instead of taking him along to the corner store and letting him chase a cat if he wants to. I'd always thought of the quality of simplicity and gaiety Molly has as being something she'd never lose, no matter how old she gets, but I wasn't so sure as she turned out of herself just then and looked around at me. She seemed to have come a long journey back from somewhere I'd never been, and to have aged a lot while she was there, in the same way that Courtney was older.

"I ought to go to bed," she said abruptly. "But do you know what's going to be the hardest part of all this to take?"

I shook my head.

"It's all the people who're going to be so kind to me to my face and then say 'I told you so—these hit-and-run war marriages . . . none of them last.'"

She got up quickly, went over to the window and stood looking out a long time before she turned around again.

"—I know all the things Courtney's been saying."

It was an effort for her to keep her voice evenly controlled.

"Kind friends couldn't wait to tell me. I've closed my ears and tried not to mind, because I knew very well I hadn't thrown myself at him. I didn't even know he was back when he called me up and asked if I'd have dinner that night. He said he was just off the plane, and I didn't know he was calling from New York until he was late because the train was. I sort of figured Courtney was busy and he didn't want to eat alone his first night back. Then bang in the middle of the ground beefsteak à la galloise he said, 'I was going to send you this from Natal, a couple of months ago, but I thought you'd think I was crazy.'"

She stopped for a moment.

"I haven't ever told anybody but Randy, because . . . well, I was so sure, you see. I thought, 'Okay, let them talk—they just don't know, and I do.' Because it was a radio blank. It had the date and my name and address on it, and the pencil marks were blurred where it had been folded in his pocket. It said, 'Molly, will you marry me as soon as I get back home? I've been wanting to ask you since the night I hope you remember too. My temperature's normal. This is very serious, and the only important thing that's ever happened to me.'—Just like that."

"Did you remember the night he meant?" I asked.

"Of course. It wouldn't sound very romantic to anybody else. There weren't any magnolias in the moonlight, and I guess that's one reason I didn't question it was true. Or if I'd been beautiful, or had a lot of money . . ."

19

She moved her hands in a light gesture, dismissing that.

"It was just a game of checkers in the Abbotts' game room, a few days before he left. Everybody else was playing bridge, and I didn't have money enough to play for the stakes they do, so I didn't want to cut in. Courtney said, 'Cass, why don't you play a game of checkers with the baby?' So he did. We sat on the floor in front of the fire and had a wonderful time. At least I did. I was a little worried because I thought he was stuck with me and just being sweet because Courtney told him to—even when he let her go home with some people who live near her because we weren't through with our game."

She stopped abruptly. "It sounds silly, doesn't it?"

"Not at all," I said.

"Anyway, he took me home, because he lived out this way. We shook hands at the door and said good night. He started away and then he came back and said 'Let's smoke one cigarette before I go.' So we sat on the porch and smoked a cigarette. Then he got up and said good night again. You know that funny smile of his? Well, the next day I was having lunch with Aunt downtown and I ran into Courtney waiting in the lounge. I don't know what I said, but she laughed and said, 'Darling, don't tell me you're like all the rest of them? He'll be here in a minute. I'll have to tell him he's done it again.' I realized then he'd just been making fun of me. He didn't even look around the restaurant."

She hesitated again.

"But he said she never told him I was there," she went on. "But that doesn't matter. I was so unhappy I could have died. I didn't want him to think I was a fool, so I went to Virginia with Aunt, and when I got back he was gone. He'd been calling me up at the house, but I told the maid not to tell anybody where I was. Then that's all I heard from him, except that he sent me a dollar and a half box of checkers from a toy shop in New York before he left—and a book of rules, because I don't play checkers very well."

She looked at me anxiously.

"Does this bore you sick?" she demanded. "It's all so simple . . ."

I shook my head.

"No, it doesn't, if you want to talk about it," I said.

"Well, I do, somehow," she said simply. "Anyway, that night at dinner we talked for hours, until they closed the restaurant, and then we walked home in the rain and talked after two o'clock. I guess nobody had ever really made love to me before, except Randy, and he doesn't count, and it all went to my head. He seemed to mean it. He was going away again, and . . . oh, I don't know. Time seemed too important, and it took five days to get a license here, so we went to Virginia, and they got the blood tests through in a couple of hours and we were married. He said he wanted it that way. He was sure if I was. He didn't want to go away without knowing completely that I belonged to him. It was all so quick . . . but I didn't have any doubts at all. And in the last four months I've tried not to let any creep in when I'd hear . . ."

She turned her head away quickly.

"We had just four days together, but . . . but I guess that was enough. I . . . oh, I can't bear it, Grace. I can't, I can't! I loved him so much! And now I hate him! I hate him! Oh, why did he have to——"

I went over to her and drew her down by me on the sofa.

"Stop it, Molly!" I said sharply. "Stop it right now. You're just being a fool, a complete absolute fool. Cass knew you a long time before he played checkers with you, so it isn't as if he'd run into you on a street corner and married you because he had a free Saturday night. You've certainly heard from him since he's been away, and——"

She shook her head quickly.

"But I haven't. He told me I wouldn't, because nobody was supposed to know where he was. A couple of times people came through and brought me a message, but all he ever said was for me to brush up on my checkers and he was all right. But I didn't mind that . . . but if he could let Courtney know . . ."

"Look, Molly," I said. "I'm going to the phone and call him now."

She was on her feet in an instant, her eyes blazing, her face pale, her fists tightly clenched at her sides.

"No you're not!" she cried. "If you do, I'll go somewhere else. You don't understand! I was right—in the very beginning I was right. He *was* making fun of me. Courtney knew it. Then he got down in the jungles and it looked different, and that's why he thought he was in love with me. It's Courtney he really loves—he always has. And she loves him. And I know it, and I hate them both!"

I got up.

"You go to bed," I said firmly. "Tomorrow you can decide what you're going to do——"

"I've decided already."

She was perfectly calm again.

"In fact, I've not only decided what I'm going to do—I've already done it. You may think it's awful, but I'm going to show them both I can be just as cold-blooded as they are. You haven't any idea what I've put up with from people around here the last four months."

Her eyes were blazing again suddenly, and as yellow as a topaz.

21

I managed a smile.

"Nobody's likely to think you're particularly cold-blooded, angel," I said. "So go to bed, and go to sleep."

In the doorway she turned back.

"I'm sorry, Grace," she said. "I haven't any right forcing my troubles on you and then acting this way. If you'd rather I'd go——"

"All I want you to do is go to bed," I said. "You're welcome to stay. There's a key in the top drawer of the desk over there, and you can come and go as you please. But do try to use your head. After all, Cass isn't responsible for what Courtney——"

I stopped. Sheila, lying on her stomach on the cool hearth bricks, gave a low growl and got to her feet. That usually meant someone coming up the front steps. I hadn't heard anyone, and I couldn't now, but she growled again, the hair on her back rising a little as she went through the dining room toward the front door.

4

"Is somebody coming?" Molly asked quickly.

"It's rather late for visitors."

I looked at the clock on the desk. It was twenty minutes to twelve.

"I'm going up," she said. "If it's anybody for me, I'm not here. Please, Grace. And you don't know where I am."

She slipped off her shoes and disappeared. I could hear the step half-way up that always creaks, and her door close softly, as I waited for the doorbell to ring. Sheila gave an impatient high-pitched bark and scratched at the door. It wasn't like her at all, and in that otherwise completely silent house it was a little disturbing. The doorbell isn't hard to find, and if it were there's a knocker there.

I went out into the hall and switched on the overhead light. I tried to tell myself it was probably someone not wanting to ring the bell at that time of night if I'd gone upstairs, and I knew no lights were visible from the street, with the old-fashioned solid wood shutters locked and barred in the dining room windows. I turned on the outside light, however, and reached out to take down the chain Molly had put in place when Randy had gone. As I touched it Sheila gave such a savage growl that I dropped it instantly.

It may be absurd to endow a dog with an intuition of danger, but when you're alone—except for a colored cook wrapped in primeval slumber downstairs—you come to depend on their acuter senses. Anyway, it would have taken

22

more courage than I had just then to have opened that door. I switched off the hall light instead, slipped into the dining room, unbolted the shutter on the farthest window, and opened the flap enough to peer out.

There wasn't anybody on the front stoop at all, or anybody that I could see in the radius of the light reaching out under the trees.

I closed the shutter and went back to the front door. Sheila was still sniffing and whining. Perhaps it was just a cat she didn't like, I thought. I turned the bolt and opened the door. She shot out in front of me, growling. I looked quickly along the street. The red tail lights of a car going a little on the diagonal straightened and went on as she dashed down the steps, nose to the bricks, following a scent that brought her to an abrupt stop at an open place on the curb four houses down. She sniffed around and came back to it, and back to the door again. I watched her, completely bewildered, as she went back to the curb, and suddenly lifted her head and howled. It was that long low howl that some people think is a warning of death . . . reeking in a dog's nostrils before mortals are aware of its chilling shadow lengthening across the doorway. I don't believe that, but I shivered a little, thinking that Lilac might hear it, and remembering her agony when a picture fell, long ago, one evening just at dusk, and the next day two little boys and she and I began to carry on by ourselves in that same house.

I also found myself glancing down the block and across the street at the yellow brick house where Colonel Primrose lives. Seven generations of John Primroses have been born and lived in that house, but fortunately only one of Sergeant Bucks. I don't know where he was born, or if he was born at all. It's hard to imagine he was ever a baby lisping at his mother's knee. It's easier to think of him as hacked full-grown out of a stone quarry. Still, it was always rather comforting to know they were both just across the way.

Or it was until I remembered they weren't there. They'd gone out of town on account of the heat. Or that's what Sergeant Buck told Lilac, and the newspapers ostensibly confirmed it. It was the first time, however, I'd ever heard of Colonel Primrose announcing his holidays publicly, and since his job is that of a special and apparently unofficial investigator for various of the Intelligence branches, it's always a little hard to tell. All I know is that he once gave me a telephone number I was to learn and destroy, so that if I ever needed him and he didn't appear to be at home I could get him. I've never used it, but I thought of it now as I whistled for Sheila.

She came reluctantly back, and I pulled her inside and closed the door, double-locking it and putting the chain up,

23

to keep something dark and amorphous that Sheila still felt —and that I was beginning to feel—out of our lives if I could.

I turned off the sitting room lights and went upstairs. Molly's door was closed. I opened it quietly, so she could get whatever conceivable breath of air might possibly stir a little later. There was none just then. I opened the door from the front bedroom through the bath into her room, and looked in. She was lying on top of the turned-down muslin spread, fast asleep, the moonlight from the open windows over the garden streaming full on her. My heart felt cold for an instant. Then I realized how jittery I really was. It was the silver glow of the moon that made her look so strange and not of this earth. The light that glistened on her upturned face was from the tears that hadn't dried as she'd cried herself to sleep. She was still fully dressed, one shoe on and the other half falling off the foot of the bed. Her bag was still unopened on the luggage rack in front of the fireplace.

I turned away. She might try to be as cold-blooded as Courtney Durbin probably was, and as Cass Crane appeared to be . . . but it was going to take a lot of the now classical blood, sweat and tears.

Something half waked me once, after I got to sleep. It sounded like a shoe dropping, and I remember thinking vaguely of Molly's shoe on the edge of the bed, and that I should have taken it off and put it on the floor, before I turned over and went back to sleep to the monotonous whirr of the electric fan out in the hall. Then something waked me again, I don't know how long after. I opened my eyes and lay there listening, unable to sort out the disturbed realities of the borderline worlds merging into each other. Then I sat up. The downstairs phone was ringing. The one on my bedside table I'd turned off, so I could sleep in the morning when it was cool. I reached out, picked it up and said "Hello," knowing, some way, before I did, that it would be Cass Crane.

"Grace?" a voice said.

It wasn't Cass. It was Randy Fleming.

"Look, Grace. Is . . . Molly all right?"

With the illuminated hands of the clock on the table standing at ten minutes past three, not even the overtone of acute anxiety evident across the wire kept me from a sharp feeling of irritation. I could be sympathetic enough with Randy's concern for her, and think it was sweet, in the daytime. To be waked up by it in the middle of a filthy hot night, with no telling when I'd get back to sleep again, was something else.

"She's perfectly all right," I said, trying not to sound as an-

I noyed as I felt. "She's fast asleep, and so was I. Now will you please go to bed, and don't worry."

Then I said, "Have you heard anything from Cass?"

I don't know why I thought he might have, or why I asked it, except that I was wide awake and curious.

"Yeah," he said shortly. "In fact, I've seen him. Sorry I woke you. Good night."

His voice couldn't have been more abrupt, nor could the phone zinging away where his voice had been. I put it down and sat there, hot, sticky and pretty mad. I knew if I turned on the light and tried to read I'd have a thousand bugs sifting in through the screen, so I kicked off the sheet and lay down again. After a few minutes I sat up, something sifting in through the screens of my own mind. Whether it was the anxiety in Randy's voice, or a feeling I'd been too short with him, I don't know. Anyway, I got up. The phone might have waked Molly, and she might have heard Cass's name.

I turned on the light and went out into the hall. There was no sound except Sheila's tail thwacking against the floor down the hall when she heard me. I looked at Molly's door. It was closed, so she probably hadn't heard the phone at all. I started back to my room. The heat was so oppressive, however, that I changed my mind and started downstairs, where it would be a little cooler.

Perhaps it was the fact that Sheila was sitting in front of the door, when she usually spends the night sprawled out on the hearth stones, that made me notice the chain had been moved . . . or it may have been that the light glinted on its polished links hanging down instead of looped up in the socket. I stopped half-way down the stairs, looked up at Molly's door, went back up, opened it quietly and looked in.

The bed was empty and she was gone, her bag still on the luggage racked in front of the fireplace.

That, I thought, was that. A couple of hours of sleep had done its job, and she'd gone home to Cass. I realized then that that was what I'd been counting on. And I was more relieved than I'd thought I'd be. It's always such a mess getting mixed up in other people's domestic quarrels. And Molly belonged with Cass. She must have been acutely aware of it, waking up and lying there alone, before she slipped out through the darkened streets and back to him.

The air probably just seemed fresher and lighter as I went back to bed. It was certainly hot enough the next morning. I woke up with the sun streaming through the windows and Lilac's heavy step plodding up the stairs. She wasn't muttering darkly to herself, so we were headed for a peaceful day, I thought as I sat up and looked at the clock. It was ten minutes to eight. I turned to smile at her polished ebony face

25

in the doorway; and my jaw dropped, but literally, as I stared blankly past her.

Molly Crane was there in the hall. She was dressed in her blue nurse's aide uniform, with her hair brushed up on the top of her head, the curling tendrils around her neck still wet from the shower. Her suntanned face was fresh and lineless, her lips bright red and smiling. Her amber eyes were a little pale, but it could so easily have been the heat that for a moment I wasn't sure it hadn't affected me myself.

She laughed. "Don't tell me you forgot I was here. I tried to be as quiet as I could."

I didn't know what to say, under the circumstances. She obviously had no idea I knew she'd been out, and apparently had a definite reason for wanting me to think she hadn't. It was very confusing. But she didn't wait for me to answer.

"I've got to be at the hospital by eight-thirty," she said. "If . . . anyone should call me, will you tell them I'll be back after lunch? If I may come back . . . do you *not* mind, really?"

Lilac stopped closing the outside shutters. "No, child, Mis' Grace she don' mind. It's company for her. She like company in the house."

As I didn't need to say anything, with Lilac taking over, I just smiled.

"Goodbye, then—I'll see you," Molly said. She went out, Lilac following her.

I poured a cup of coffee, turned on the portable radio on the table for the eight o'clock local news, and glanced through the comic strips waiting for it to come on. When it did come there wasn't much I hadn't heard the evening before. I turned to the gossip column. The last paragraph stood out from the rest of it.

"We can hardly call it this column's scoop, because it's what everybody's been saying since they caught their breath again. But unless our crystal ball is cloudy with the heat, we see a low pressure area reaching as far west as Reno. Some people say he forgot to tell her he was coming back last night, but he looked cheerful enough when we saw him being met by one of the Capital's coolest looking lovelies . . . who may, of course, just have happened along. You know how airports are, these days. You're apt to run into most anybody."

I turned the page and took up my orange juice, half listening to the commercial reporter announcing that the Snow White Laundry was discontinuing pickup and delivery and would take no more new customers, and Fur Storage Inc. had no room for more furs or woolens. You know how it is

. . . the radio goes on, and your inner ears are partly closed. Then mine were abruptly open.

". . . corner of 26th and Beall Streets in Georgetown this morning," the voice was saying.

I put my glass down and sat up, trying to grope back into the lost ether for what had gone before.

"—The police were called by a paper carrier who noticed the front door standing open and looked inside. The body was taken to the Gallinger Hospital, where the cause of death will be determined. Officers of the Homicide Squad said there was no evidence of violence, but the circumstances surrounding the case were such that an investigation will be made. If you are unable to find your usual supply of Mullher's Five-X Beer at your dealer's . . ."

I switched off the dial and sat there, staring blankly in front of me. I couldn't bring back the words I'd missed . . . but I could hear Randy Fleming as plain as if he were in the room speaking to me. And I could hear the tone of his voice. "Yeah . . . In fact, I've seen him . . ."

"—Mis' Grace?"

I looked around with a start. Lilac was in the doorway.

"Mis' Grace—Colonel Primrose, he downstairs. He says, don' you hurry yourself none, but he want to see you if it ain' inconvenient."

5

There have been times when I've been glad to see Colonel Primrose, and no doubt there will be again . . . but this was not one of them.

Normally, I have no reluctance about murder, but the more the details of the night before reconstructed themselves in my mind the less I found myself wanting to be in anyway involved with anything that might have happened on 26th and Beall Streets. As I came into the sitting room and looked out into the garden, however, and saw his solid, slightly rotund figure in white linen, he looked so much more like the county agent inspecting the tomato vines than a sub rosa policeman that it occurred to me suddenly that might not be why he was here at all.

He came to the back hall door and inside, smiling as if the idea of murder had never been remotely in his mind.

"What kind of a spray are you using, if any, Mrs. Latham?" he asked amiably.

"Nicotine, I think, was the last one," I said.

I looked at the perforated leaf he had in his hand. The tip was curled down with some kind of blight, and the whole

27

thing looked pretty discouraging, frankly. I changed the subject.

"Anyway, I thought you were out of town," I said. Then I said, "But look at you! What have you been doing . . . haunting a house?"

The shoulder of his white linen suit had a great black cobweb streaked over it, and there was another down the side of his trousers leg, which also had a jagged tear in it.

He cocked his head down and around—he can't turn it normally because of a bullet he stopped in the last war—and looked at himself.

"I've just been in one," he said. "If it wasn't haunted before, it ought to be now. You know that empty hovel on the corner next to the Cass Cranes'?"

I stood looking at him blankly. ". . . the corner of 26th and Beall Streets," the radio reporter had said. But that wasn't the Cranes' house at all. It was the empty tumbledown shack next door to them. And if it wasn't the Cranes' house, it obviously wasn't Cass they'd found in it. I walked to a chair and sat down abruptly, so relieved that I don't think my knees would have continued to support me!

He was looking at me with a quizzical but rather perturbed interest. "—Do you know something about this business, Mrs. Latham?"

"I don't even know what business you're talking about," I said. "I just heard the end of a broadcast this morning, and I thought something unpleasant had happened at the Cranes', is all."

"Why did you think that?"

"No reason—except the location."

"Then you don't know whose body was found there?"

He was looking at me with odd intentness.

I shook my head.

"Do you know who this is?"

He reached in his inside coat pocket, took out a small oblong leather folder and handed it to me. It was a public vehicle driver's identification, issued in New York City . . . the kind you see in taxicabs, with a usually unrecognizable picture on it of the man sitting in the front. I looked at it, and at Colonel Primrose.

"—This is that queer little creature who drives for Mr. Durbin, isn't it?"

He nodded.

"It was his body found in the house next to the Cranes'."

It may have been wrong of me, but it seemed a little strange, somehow, that Colonel Primrose should have been so disturbed, as he patently was, about such an odd little creature. After all, when the papers say we've lost two Flying Fortresses it can hardly mean anything except that twenty of our best have probably gone. We seem to think so little in terms of individual lives any more, and Colonel Primrose had been where better men than this died by the thousands, in the last war.

I handed it back to him.

"I'm sorry," I said. "What happened, do you know?"

He hesitated for just an instant.

"The body was carried in there. He died somewhere else."

"How do you know——"

He smiled patiently.

"The dust on those floors is a quarter of an inch thick, Mrs. Latham. The body didn't move after it was put down. The footprints from the front door were made by a man with feet twice the size of his. And in stocking feet. He caught his foot on a nail on the floor and left a thread of his sock. The police have it. Furthermore, the little man had been drinking whisky . . . with a strong base of nicotine. Enough to kill him about fifty times."

He raised the leaf from my tomato plant to his nose and sniffed at it. I stared at him with my mouth open, and I mean it literally.

"Why, Colonel Primrose!" I gasped. "You don't mean you think——"

He smiled a little wryly.

"Think you poisoned him? No, my dear. I don't think you did. But I think somebody with a Victory garden in the back yard could have . . . and there's quite a nice one at the Cranes', next door. I saw it over the fence."

I sat there pretty stunned for a moment or two. But it seemed so preposterous.

"Why in heaven's name would any of them want to kill that little man?" I demanded. "It's . . . it's absurd!"

"I'm wondering if it is," he said calmly. He got up and went over to the fireplace where I keep the big parlor matches, and was lighting a cigar. It seemed to take a very long time. When he turned around his face was soberer than I'd ever seen it.

"I want you to do something for me, Mrs. Latham," he said quietly. "I want you to go upstairs and pack your bag, and leave Washington . . . without telling anybody but me where you're going. I'll have Buck drive you to Baltimore to take a train."

It must have been one of my blanker mornings, because it seemed to me all I'd done since I woke up was stare at somebody like an idiot child.

"Why on earth . . . ?" I demanded.

"Because I don't want you hurt," he said.

He hesitated a moment.

"I don't know as much about this as I'd like to, my dear

. . . but it looks serious. And it looks as if you've stepped right into it. I'm afraid you probably don't know anything about it on the one hand, and may know altogether too much on the other. Won't you, just for once, believe what I'm telling you, and believe that if you didn't mean as much to me as——"

"Is this what brought you over here this morning, Colonel?" I asked. It seemed a little early in the morning for all this, and I do have my duty toward Sergeant Buck. "—Or why did you come?"

He drew a deep breath.

"I had some idea, Mrs. Latham, of finding out what a man whose body was dumped in a hovel in Beall Street was doing on your doorstep at twenty minutes to twelve last night."

"*My* doorstep?"

He nodded.

"A police patrol car keeping an eye on my house saw him. He ran when you turned on the light. His car was just down the street, and he got in and drove away. You came out on the porch a minute later."

He smiled rather grimly.

"You probably know that. They got his number, and stood by here in case he came back. Then they picked up the car, parked on O Street near 26th, at four-fifteen this morning. He was dead—as far as they can figure in this weather—between two and three. Not later, anyway."

He stopped and looked at me intently. "I'd like to know why he was here."

"I wish I could tell you," I said, truthfully. "But I haven't the foggiest idea in the world. Unless—you'll find this out if you don't already know, so I may as well tell you—it was because Molly Crane spent the night here. And I don't——"

"Is that Cass Crane's wife?"

I nodded.

His black parrot's eyes sparkled. "Why was she staying here?"

He asked it so curtly that I wondered if he'd got himself mixed up with Sergeant Buck. Buck is the really military member of the family.

"Something happened," I said. "Cass didn't let her know he was coming home, or something. She was hurt, and mad, so she . . ."

I broke off abruptly. "And now you'll decide Molly was trying to poison Cass. Do you know, Colonel Primrose, that much as I enjoy knowing you, sometimes I wish I didn't?"

Whatever he would have said to that was stopped by Lilac's appearance.

"—Mr. Gofiel says he got some meat in, but he won' have none long if you 'spect to get any. Here's your book."

"All right," I said. I took the ration book.

"And don' you stop and talk all day and get there late. He ain' goin' to save nothin' past ten o'clock."

She gave Colonel Primrose an unfriendly glance and waddled back down to the kitchen.

"I'm sorry, Colonel," I said. "Murder's one thing, but lamb chops are another. So if you don't mind . . ."

I picked up my hat and bag.

"There's one thing, however. I don't know what you're talking about, about my having got into something . . . but I'm not going away. If my child should get leave before he goes across somewhere, he'll want to come home and I want to be here."

I looked at my dog-eared ration book. "And I've got to go."

I left him standing in front of the house, still smoking his cigar, annoyed and more worried about the death of Mr. Durbin's troglodyte handy man than seemed to me to make much sense. If he had, as I did, to feed two people on one ration book, he'd have something to be concerned about, I thought as I headed for the market on Wisconsin Avenue. Lilac's books, as pristine and untouched as the unclipped coupons in millionaires' safety deposit vaults, lie in a box on the bureau, with her insurance policies, her marriage license, and the deed to the cemetery plot. No efforts of mine to explain that the $10,000 fine mentioned on the back of them is not for their use but their misuse have had the slightest effect. She's only threatened to leave me twice. The first time was when I tried to insist she use her coupons, the second was when I tried to get her to take mine to the store. And since I'd rather eat chicken till I fly and fish till I swim, and go after both, there was no real problem involved.

As I turned the corner toward Mr. Scofield's, I saw it was not to be without its compensations. When, otherwise, would I ever have seen Corinne Blodgett's ample white derriere backing down the steps of a street car as if they were a fireman's ladder, dropping her string shopping bag and holding up what little traffic there was while she rescued a one-point red coupon that had fluttered out of the sheaf of ration books she was holding tightly between her teeth? The marines landing on New Georgia never had the beaming consciousness of triumph that Corinne had, finally making the curb in front of Mr. Scofield's dingy-looking market. But most of the marines, probably, hadn't spent their lives in broadcloth-upholstered limousines.

"My dear, I'm enchanted!" Corinne cried. She got her various appendages together, straightened her big white straw hat and mopped her streaming face. "The man couldn't have been nicer. He gave me a pass for a dollar and a quarter and told me I could ride *free,* on any bus or street car I

31

wanted to, for a *week!* Now my dear, you know that's a lot cheaper than keeping a car and paying that awful man I had a hundred dollars a month just to drive around and open doors. You know it is, Grace, and feeding him too. My dear, I tell you I think we're all going to learn of lots of things. And my dear, I sat next to the loveliest little woman! She says if you buy a piece of beef and cook it with okra and tomatoes, and things, and put it in jars, you have vegetable soup all winter. And my dear——"

She stopped abruptly half inside the door. It was not unlike the Queen Mary deciding to reverse engines in the middle of the Potomac Basin.

"—Have you heard about that poor little creature that drives for Mr. Durbin? My dear, he's dead! It's the most extraordinary thing. Why, do you know——"

"Excuse me, ma'am."

A delivery boy with a box of groceries on his shoulder was waiting patiently to get out.

"Oh, I'm being a bottle-neck!" Corinne laughed. She went on full sail into the store. "I was saying, my dear, literally *nobody* can understand it. Mr. Durbin was so dependent on him, and everybody thought he was really devoted to him, in his way. And I must remember to tell him about the streetcars. But, my dear, there it is. Nobody can imagine why he ever did it. Do you suppose this is any good?"

I stared at her past the head of lettuce she was holding up.

"—Did what, Corinne?" I demanded.

"Oh, my dear, don't you know? He killed himself. Courtney says poor Mr. Durbin was so cut up about it. She thinks it was because he'd been drinking quite a lot. Mr. Durbin had said he was going to have him deported, or something, but it was just to make him pull himself together."

"Oh," I said.

"You didn't think I meant Mr. Durbin had done it? But that's just silly, dear, because a good driver is practically impossible to replace, these days.—Of course, it didn't surprise me, Grace, because the Swami said there was blood on the moon, and he looked straight at Courtney . . ."

"Swami?" I protested feebly. If there's anybody who doesn't look like my idea of a swami—gleaned, I admit, from hawknosed people with turbans and crystal balls in tea rooms—it's Duleep Singh. And I hadn't noticed he was looking at Courtney, though he had been at Molly Crane.

"Well, I don't know whether he's a swami or not," Corinne said. "But you can't call him 'Mahatma' because he wears clothes. I think 'Mr. Singh' sounds absurd, and he certainly knows things ordinary people don't know. Just take last night. He knew something was going to happen and it did. The first time he came to our house I'd been telling Horace about him, and you know how Horace is. Dry as dust, and so literal you can't even say it looks like rain."

She gathered up a half dozen yellow squash and put them in her basket.

"Horace hates squash," she remarked. "But he needs yellow food. Anyway, that night, my dear, he said to Duleep Singh, 'My wife says you can read the future.' My dear, I could have killed him. But Duleep Singh just said, 'May I suggest you look carefully before you go into the venture you were considering as I came into the room.'"

Corinne was carefully picking out a couple of yellow cucumbers from under the pile of fresh green ones. She turned back to me.

"My dear, I can't tell you. Horace was undone. He literally was. If the Chief Justice had turned a handspring Horace couldn't have been more reduced. There have been times when I've thought Horace was the reincarnation of something fed on papyrus, but really . . ."

She wiped a tear of laughter out of one eye.

"That was less than two months ago, and Horace still isn't the same. Of course, he never tells me anything about his business, so I don't know what it was, *but*, my dear . . ."

Most people lower their voices when they are about to impart the climax of a story in the grocery store, but not Corinne.

"—*Yesterday*, he had a séance with the Swami. Horace Blodgett! Would you ever have believed it?"

She stopped and waited, not without drama.

"No, I really wouldn't," I said.

"Nor would I," she said firmly. "But he did, and he'd die if he knew I knew it. He told me he was bringing his sister to tea, because he knows that's the *one* way to get me out of the house. But he didn't know she'd gone to Middleburg and didn't tell him because he doesn't approve of anyone using gas for pleasure-driving. But her cook told mine. And then, my dear, he sneaked in the back way, and let the Swami in himself. Then, afterwards, he sneaked out again and came in the front door, pretending he'd just got home and his sister couldn't come. So I pretended I'd just come in too."

She straightened her hat that had got knocked awry as she fished around under some sacks hunting for potatoes.

"And of course, Grace, I don't mind. I've so often thought Horace's soul was like a newt's, a nice newt's, not really developed yet, and if he feels finally that he needs help he can make the house a rat race if he likes. I'm just too glad to think he's at last embracing the fuller life."

She turned around. "Mr. Scofield, why do you charge twenty-three points for a can of pineapples?—Of course, my dear, I still don't see what Cass Crane's coming home had to do with it. Or why Horace had to say he didn't know Cass was coming, when I distinctly heard him say so when he let the Swami out.—Here, dear, do you mind counting up and seeing if I have enough coupons to buy a can of sardines for the cat."

She was off, holding out her book to the harassed spinster taking a man's place behind the counter. She waved to me as I went out with a pound of lamb for stew. Poor Mr. Scofield was trying to add up her points. There'll have to be a psychiatric hospital for grocers and butchers, before the war is over, and Corinne Blodgett ought to help endow it handsomely.

.   .

6

Of course it was a wonderful commentary on Washington, the small town where nobody gets away with anything very long. Horace Blodgett should have known it better than anyone else, if just for the number of Congressional hearings he's sat at, beside clients who didn't know that last month's dinner party they'd kept off the society page would be front page news in a few weeks. Transposing Corinne's story into reasonable terms, it was perfectly obvious that Horace Blodgett, corporation lawyer and a man of considerable behind-the-scenes importance, newt of soul as he might be, was having a plain business conference with Duleep Singh, member of an accredited economic mission to the United States. Also, that it was very hush-hush. It wasn't the fuller life Horace was pursuing, but the richer life, for one of his clients and himself, and anyone could safely say it wasn't God but Mammon presiding. It was a little amusing, as a matter of fact, to see Horace caught in the toils he'd been warning the unwary about for years. I suppose you have to know him to understand it. He's so meticulous.

I was thinking about them as I went back home. Horace Blodgett came from fine, well-to-do, waste-not want-not Quaker stock, went to a rigorous Quaker college and a law school and stepped into a ready-made place in his father's firm. His life with one exception was in the same strictly formal pattern. The exception was his marriage to Corinne. I'd always thought that, true to himself and his training, he'd combined wild oats and the primrose path within the letter of the law. Corinne was beautiful, mad as a hatter in a merry way, not as she is now, and nobody could possibly see what she saw in him. I remember seeing them when I was still a child. She was lovely and lots of fun, and he already seemed mummified to me. The next shock was the child they pro-

34

duced. She had violet eyes and milk-white skin and a mass of flaming gold curls that was unbelievable. She was simply dazzling. She couldn't help being spoiled rotten, because it was like having a child goddess growing up in the house. I remember her well—she was just six years younger than I— and I remember the shock of their coming back without her when they took a trip around the world the year after she came out. They took her because she was besieged with men who wanted to marry her, and Horace was still a Quaker at heart. Just what happened, except that she met a man on a tramp steamer they were on in some out of the way place, and married him two or three days later, I don't know.

The Blodgetts came home, and nobody saw them out anywhere for quite a while. Horace made a couple of trips out to see her, and on the last one he brought her body back. She'd had some tropical disease and was being taken to the nearest town with an American hospital when the car skidded on a mountain road.

That was fifteen years ago, and it was when Corinne began to change. It was a tragic thing, but in a sense the girl's actual physical death seemed to make it easier for both of them. Horace went on being dry as dust again, and Corinne developed a kind of amnesia and became what she is now, taking up whatever fad comes along, with Horace watching her with a dry flicker in his eye, never annoyed or bored or even irritated with her, or showing the least concern for her extravagance.

—Or so I'd have thought until I answered the phone just as I finished lunch a few hours later. I didn't recognize Corinne's voice for a long instant. She was whispering into the mouthpiece, and I'd never heard Corinne Blodgett whisper before.

"Grace, listen to me?" she said desperately. "You're not to repeat what I said this morning! Horace is furious at me, he says I'll ruin him! My dear, he's almost beside himself. He doesn't know I told you, and don't tell a soul, Grace!"

I could hardly believe it was Corinne I was listening to.

"Of course I won't," I said quickly. "Don't be silly. I wouldn't have thought of it anyway."

"But you don't understand. I don't myself—but I've done something *terrible!*"

She was so upset that she was half crying.

"Nobody else could have heard me, could they, dear?"

Then her voice changed abruptly, and became normal and childishly gay and a little dégagé.

"—Thank you, dear. It's sweet of you to ask me. I'll be over about five, dear. If it's for China Relief you know how interested I am. Goodbye, dear."

I blinked a little as the phone zinged in my ear. I wouldn't have thought Corinne capable of so much guile. I could almost see Horace coming into the room behind her . . . but as for seeing him furious or beside himself, throwing her into the state of abject desperation she was in, my mind was a complete blank. And as for nobody else having heard her in the store, I couldn't imagine that either, unless all Mr. Scofield's customers that morning were deaf as monoliths.

I sat there trying to recall who, if anybody, we knew, or who might know her, had been there. The faces were all blurred in my mind. I'd been too occupied listening to her myself, and trying to figure my own ration book. The only person I could remember seeing that I knew was Julie Ross. I'd smiled at her as I was waiting at the meat counter, but whether she'd been there when Corinne was talking, or had come in later, I hadn't noticed.

It was very distressing . . . and also, I thought, rather odd. It was evident that what Corinne had done was important, some way. Horace Blodgett wouldn't be raising hell, and Corinne wouldn't have called up as she did if she hadn't been really terrified. And the crux of the whole thing was obviously Cass Crane. I wondered about that. It threw a new light on Duleep Singh's absorbed fascination in Molly Crane the night before at the Abbotts', and what seemed to me now his almost deliberate setting Courtney and Molly at each other's throat. Unless, I thought, I was—like Corinne—making a swami out of just an extremely shrewd man of the world. The only even figurative blood on the moon had turned out to be the little troglodyte's, and it seemed hard to believe Duleep Singh would concern himself with such small deer.

It was at that point that I thought of the little driver and D. J. Durbin waiting at the dead end of the road outside the Abbotts', and his rescuing Mr. Durbin from the black cat. It was himself he should have saved, I thought. Then I remembered D. J. Durbin scanning the skies, and the plane coming over. He must have known Cass was coming back, too. I tried to think of the people at the Abbotts' who did know, for certain. Courtney, and Duleep Singh, and Horace Blodgett who was on the other side of the garden with Mr. Abbott. In fact, Molly was about the only one who mattered that didn't know, it seemed to me.

Lilac was taking my lunch tray downstairs.

"Did anyone call Miss Molly while I was out this morning?" I asked.

She stopped in the doorway.

"Her *husban'* didn't call her, if that's what you're askin'," she said darkly. "Ain' nobody call her, 'cept Mis' Courtney. She call her. I said she weren't here an' I ain' seen her. What's she call up for? She still hungerin' after that child's husband?"

36

I'm afraid there aren't many things going on that Lilac doesn't know about. The grapevine in the basement is much more efficient, some way, than the telephone. I ignored the question, wondering myself why Courtney Durbin had called Molly, and how she knew she was there.

"Have you heard anything about the man they found down there this morning?" I asked.

"You mean the man that was daid?"

I nodded.

"Ain' heard nothin'," Lilac said, calmly. " 'Ceptin' he was daid when Mr. Randy put him in there."

I turned around.

"Lilac—what *are* you saying?"

"I ain' sayin' nothin' more," she said flatly, and plodded downstairs, mumbling to herself.

Well, I just don't know. To say I sat there speechless is not even understatement. It doesn't make any sense. I was stunned, literally, as Corinne would say. The room seemed to be going in circles around me. And I knew I couldn't go down to the kitchen and ask Lilac what in heaven's name she meant, because she'd said it as plainly as anybody could. She'd also said she wasn't saying nothin' more, and I knew what that meant. It meant she wasn't saying anything, and I knew there wasn't any use trying to make her.

I just sat there. The mere question of what Randy, who lives in Chevy Chase, was doing on 26th and Beall Streets after two or three o'clock in the morning, which was when Colonel Primrose had said the little man died, was hard enough. But moving a dead body into an empty house . . . And I couldn't tell myself it wasn't true. If Lilac said it, she said it knowing it was so. I could have doubted the coffee table in front of me with more sense.

Some kind of answers kept sifting into my consciousness. Randy Fleming was in love with Molly, everybody knew that. And he'd gone back to the house. But it wasn't the little man he'd gone back to see, it was Cass Crane. The little man had somehow got in the way . . .

I got up and moved across the room and sat down again. I didn't believe that, really. Not of Randy. He just wasn't that kind. He could have hit Cass in the jaw and knocked him down, and his head might have hit a fender, but he wouldn't conceivably have set out cold-bloodedly . . .

I stopped abruptly and sat there suddenly quiet, a pretty ghastly hollow in the pit of my stomach. "—I've already done it . . . I'll show them both I can be as cold-blooded as they are . . ."

Hearing those words echo back from the night before drowned out any other sound. I thought for a moment it was something I was projecting out of myself that just seemed to be Molly Crane standing in the hall doorway, her blue nurse's aide uniform rumpled as if she'd been working in it all morning, the smile on her face fading to a puzzled question, her red lips parted a little, her amber eyes still widening.

"Grace—what's the matter?" she said quickly. "Don't you feel well? Eat some salt, quick."

I shook my head, trying to clear it.

"I'm all right."

She took a step forward.

"You haven't heard from . . . Cass, have you?"

I think that wasn't what she started to say, but maybe it was. I shook my head.

"No, I haven't. Have you?"

"Yes."

She turned her head away a little so I couldn't see her face for an instant.

"He called up the hospital this morning. He's having lunch with Courtney this noon."

"He *what?*" I demanded blankly. "Molly, what on earth goes on? I mean——"

"Oh, she asked me too. Sweet, wasn't it. Cass said he had to go. He wanted to come out to the hospital and get me, but I had to help with an operation at half-past twelve. He had to report this morning to the BEW and the War Department. So he was tied up till then. He said it was business, and I'm . . . I'm trying to believe him. He said he tried to find me last night, but nobody knew where I was."

"Did you say why he didn't let you know he was coming?" I asked gently.

She shook her head. "He said Courtney told him I was at the Abbotts' with Randy but . . . he called Randy, and Randy said he didn't know where I was. I made him promise not to tell. I was . . . I mean, I was terribly hurt . . ."

"I know," I said.

"He was sort of stiff about it, as if it was my fault."

"Look, Molly," I said. "Did you *tell* him you didn't know he was coming?"

She shook her head again.

"No, because . . ."

I must have sounded a little grim, I'm afraid.

"Molly . . . aren't you being a stiff-necked little fool, if you'll let me say so? Because you didn't want him to think you cared that much . . ."

"Maybe I am," she said quickly. "But if he could let her know, he could let me. And she wasn't the only one. Julie Ross knew. Mrs. Blodgett knew. She said at supper she knew I'd be glad when he got home, but I thought she just meant generally, because she thinks I see too much of Randy.

38

You know how vague she is. So he could have let me know if he'd wanted to."

I looked at her, trying to believe there was nothing deeper on her mind than this. If I hadn't known she'd been out at ten minutes past three that morning, it would have been different. I wondered for an instant if she'd seen Cass, but I didn't think so. And she couldn't have seen Randy, or he wouldn't have called me up. Unless . . . he'd seen her, and thought she was back, and was trying —it was in my mind so I might as well admit it—to establish an alibi for her. But that was pretty far-fetched. I suppose I should have had courage to ask her frankly, but I didn't.

"Courtney phoned and asked me to come to lunch," she was saying evenly. "She said it was absurd for me and Cass to be quarrelling, and stupid of me to be jealous of their friendship."

"And what did you say?"

"I said thanks, I thought it was frightfully sweet of her, and if I could possibly get around I'd adore to, and I was dreadfully sorry to read in the paper that Achille was dead— which is true, I am—and that's all. Sometimes I think she's just trying to make me quarrel with her. I've got a stinking temper, and I'd say a lot of things I shouldn't say. She's got the advantage . . . but I'm not going to give anybody the satisfaction of knowing I can't take it on the chin if I have to."

"She hasn't got the advantage, darling," I said calmly. "You've got it. Every woman married to a man has it, if she's even half-way bright."

She shook her head.

"Not me. Maybe I could make him forget her for a little while if I tried to, but that isn't the point. I want all or nothing—freely or not at all. If it was war hysteria I want to know it, now. And I'm not going to put a shawl on my head and be the little woman weeping and saying Darling, how could you forget! You can call it . . . stubbornness, or anything you like, but that's the way it is. I just don't want him ever to know how like broken-up jelly I feel inside."

She stared up at the ceiling for an instant, her eyes very wide open. Then she took a quick deep breath and looked back at me with an effort to smile and brush it off as inconsequential.

"Do you mind going over to the house with me? I have to get a dress, and I'd better show, I think. Your friend Colonel Primrose asked me if I could be there at three o'clock."

"Oh, dear," I thought. I said, "Why don't you go by yourself? Maybe Cass will be there, and you'll have a chance to get this straightened out."

"That's what I've been trying to tell you, Grace," she answered calmly. "I can say all this, but I know if he touched me, even once, I'd . . . I'd crawl back, the way women always do. And I'd hate myself. Don't look at me that way, Grace . . . I know I sound childish. But if he could make me as blind as . . . I seem to have been, then I'd always doubt any happiness I had. I'd never be sure."

She smiled. "—Please come. What is it they used to say . . . save me from myself."

"All right," I said. "I'll save you from yourself. But I think you'd be a lot wiser if you'd let yourself go. You don't mind if I take Sheila, do you? She doesn't get out much, with the rabies quarantine."

I put the muzzle and leash on Sheila while Molly went upstairs and changed into the tan cotton dress she'd worn over the night before. As I waited for her the business of Randy Fleming came back with a kind of benumbing impact. It was so unbelievable. And there was one thing I thought she ought to know . . .

"Do you know Colonel Primrose?" I asked, approaching it obliquely, as we went along P Street to the corner.

"Just barely. Cass knows him."

She added, "I suppose he's looking into Achille's . . . death, isn't he?"

For a second my blood chilled. Her hesitation before she didn't say "murder" was almost as disturbing as anything that had gone before.

"The paper said he drank some poisoned liquor," she added. "It seems a curious thing to have around.—Hello, Julie."

We were going down 28th Street. I glanced around. Julie Ross was out on her front porch with a broom sweeping off the steps.

"Hello, Molly. Hello, Grace," she said. "Come on in."

"Can't, darling, we're going over to my place. We're being investigated by the Gestapo. See you later."

Julie Ross looked back into the house, her big dark eyes suddenly changing. She came down toward us.

"Come on in—just a second," she said urgently. "Please—for God's sake. That's what I want to talk to you about. I'm almost out of my mind."

7

We hesitated for a moment.

"Gosh, everybody seems to be in trouble today," Molly said with sudden feeling. "It must be sun spots. Hurry up, darling, we've really got to go."

We went up into the long double room. It's a lovely room, all lime-yellow and dusty pinkish gray and white, and a perfect background for Julie Ross's almost Latin type.

"Just a second," she said. "I've got to——"

She ran up to the head of the stairs and stood for an instant, listening. Then she came back down.

"—You know those two men I had over at Molly's last night?"

It was me she was speaking to. I nodded. "Mr. Austin and Mr. Sondauer."

"No, no, his name's Skagerlund, Louis Skagerlund. Anyway, a friend of mine called up last week and said two old friends of hers were trying to find a quiet place with a garden, not a hotel, and I had a lot of room and would I take them. She'd told them it would be around three hundred a month for the two—room, bath and breakfast—and would I?"

She put her hands out in a quick nervous gesture.

"Well, I'd take the devil himself for half that. I moved myself and the kids over into the servants' rooms over the kitchen and gave them the second floor. Yesterday Spud's mother came and simply raised hell. I was bringing degradation to the fair name of Ross, and they'd never approved of their son's marrying a divorced woman, and the minute he went to bleed and die for his country the mother of his defenseless little ones had to open a boarding house!"

She stepped over to the front windows, looked up and down the street, and sat down there where she could still keep her eye out.

"Anyway, last night some people dropped in, and they came home and I asked them to come out and have a drink. That's when somebody mentioned Cass, and either they knew him or they wanted to know him. That's how we got around to your house. Mr. Austin said he didn't think we ought to say we knew he was home. It was a little cockeyed, but so many things are these days. When we got back it was so damned hot I turned out the lights and went out on the terrace after they went up. I sat there thinking about Spud, and things, and all of a sudden I heard Skagerlund say, 'He would not recognize me, my friend.' His voice is sort of thick and rumbling. I realized they were just behind me, coming into the garden. I didn't know what to do, so I just closed my eyes and sat."

She glanced out of the window again, and moistened her lips with a quick movement of her tongue.

"Austin said, 'He's nobody's fool,' and Skagerlund laughed. It was a funny, short laugh. He said, 'But neither am I—I am always prepared.' Then somebody said 'Ssh!' and I heard a piece of glass crumble, and I knew they were right beside me, because somebody in that chair had dropped one earlier. And just then a dog barked, and I pretended to wake up. They came over and said it was hot, and I got some ice water. Then Mr. Skagerlund began asking all sorts of questions, about Washington, and people, and finally got around to Randy. Where he lived, and what he was doing at your house with you, Molly, and who you were, Grace."

"Well," Molly said practically, "what did you tell him?"

"I thought the best thing was to pretend I hated Randy and didn't know where he lived, and didn't want to know, and whatever he was doing at your house he was up to no good. Anyway, this morning when I made up his bed there was an automatic on the dresser. When he came in this noon I told him I'd seen it and asked him not to leave it where one of the kids could get it. He said, 'Perhaps Madame regrets having us here—would she prefer we move?' I would, of course, but I paid a lot of bills with the three hundred dollars, so I'm stuck. I said no, I loved having them—I felt so safe having a man with a gun in the house. But I don't! There's something screwy going on, and I don't know what it is—and I'm scared. Every time the phone rings they listen on the extension, and—oh gosh, here they come!"

She got up quickly. "Go out the service door, will you? Please, quick!"

A taxi had pulled up in front of the house. Molly and Sheila and I got around through the dining room and the kitchen to the service gate. We waited there until the cab had gone, and a few minutes longer, before we went out into the street and on down toward Dumbarton.

We didn't speak for a minute.

"I think there's something else she didn't tell us," Molly said then, deliberately. "But I wonder whose friends they are?"

I didn't say anything.

"*Did* Randy recognize him?" she asked.

"Yes. He said his name is Lons Sondauer. He'd met him in Cairo."

We turned into Beall Street off 27th, and we both stopped short for an instant. It was usually swarming with children, and women fanning themselves on the doorsteps. Now it was empty except for two little boys hanging curiously on the broken-down gate across from the Cranes'. That in itself must have told Colonel Primrose a silent story, I thought. I glanced up at the bedroom window of the house of a friend of Lilac's who helps us out occasionally, and saw the stringy lace curtain move as someone stepped away from it. There were probably a hundred eyes silently watching us as we went down the street. I'd expected that, and Randy should have known it the night before. But there's no static along

42

the grapevine. He'd probably thought there were no eyes to see him because he himself could see none.

A police car was standing in front of Molly's house, and a uniformed officer was leaning on the derelict fence of the house on the corner, where the body had been found. Our steps slowed down a little as we came along, across the street, toward the cars parked there.

"Well, my nurse used to say, 'I'd rather take a dose of castor oil,' " Molly said.

The effort at lightness in her voice wasn't very successful, and the radiance had gone out from under her sun tan, leaving her face a matte-dulled brown. I could have counted her heart beats, watching the pulse in her slim throat.

As we went across, the little colored boy swinging on the gate jumped off onto the sidewalk.

"I'll run your dog for a nickel, Miss," he said, grinning. "See, out there." He pointed to the open field above the Rock Creek drive. "You'll be over there, I guess. I know her." He pointed to Molly.

"Fine," I said. I handed him Sheila's leash and the two of them bounded off together.

I didn't see Sergeant Phineas T. Buck until we came around the patrol car and started up Molly's iron steps. He was standing in the open doorway of the dilapidated house on the corner. He looked very much as if he were supporting the whole works . . . Atlas in a banker's gray business suit, though I don't remember in any of the accounts I've read of Atlas's pausing to spit, as Sergeant Buck did then into the tangled grass beside the rotten steps. If everybody I know evinced the same pleasure in seeing me that was on his seamy façade just then, I'd go quietly and cut my throat. His viscid fish-gray eyes rested on me as if he wished I would, though I imagine when his lips moved sideways in his lantern jaw he was saying, "Howdedo, Ma'am," because he's always—so far—been polite to me.

"There . . . seems to be quite a crowd," Molly said calmly.

It didn't seem to have occurred to me until just then that for the police and Colonel Primrose to be inside the Cranes' house someone must have been there to let them in . . . a man's house still being his own even in Washington. So that Cass must be there. I looked quickly at Molly. Two bright spots were burning in her cheeks as she opened the screen door and stepped inside. It wouldn't have been more than three or four feet from there to the door of the double living room, but it seemed a long way and a difficult one until she was there in it.

"Hello, everybody. Hello, Cass."

Cass Crane was standing in the door between the front

43

and back rooms. He didn't move, but just stood looking at her. A psychologist I knew once did an elaborate series of tests to show that people's eyes don't, in themselves, have any expression of joy or sadness, and if the rest of the face is obliterated no one could ever tell what emotion there is behind them. I've never believed it, and I still don't, though I can't say what the emotion was in his eyes just then. Except that there was an almost brooding intensity in them, questioning, trying to understand her—or himself, who knows? —that melted into tenderness as he smiled and came across the room.

"Hello, Molly," he said quietly.

He took hold of her arms, pinioning them tightly to her sides. I could see the white knuckles on his strong sun-blackened hands. He bent his head and kissed her gently on the mouth, and raised his head again, shaking it a little at her, smiling. Then he released her arms and stepped back, and smiled at me across her shoulder.

There were four other people in the room. Only two of them were brazen enough not to have turned their heads. One was Colonel Primrose, and the other was Courtney Durbin. The police detective there was looking at his notes, and Randy Fleming was scraping a blob of paint off the hearth with the toe of his shoe. He looked up at Molly then. She'd put out her hand, steadying herself a little against the door frame. It wasn't noticeable, and she looked as if she'd been completely unresponsive. I suppose Randy knew. He looked away again, quickly, and not very happily. But just seeing him there in the flesh had a heartening effect on me . . . his tan uniform, his sandy hair and clean-cut sunburned face and his blue eyes and firm jaw. Lilac could be wrong, I thought. The grapevine can't necessarily be infallible.

Cass stood beside him at the other end of the fireplace.

"You know Colonel Primrose, Molly," he said. "This is Inspector Bigges. Mrs. Crane, Inspector, and Mrs. Latham. And you know Courtney."

The color in Molly's cheeks had gone. She spoke to Colonel Primrose and the Inspector, and turned to Courtney, sitting in a long bamboo chair with places in the arms for books and pipes that Cass had brought from his bachelor quarters. She looked cool and detached and slightly amused.

"I hope you don't mind my being here, Molly," she said. "It's not my fault. D. J. thought one of us ought to come over next door, and Colonel Primrose brought me in here."

"Oh," Molly said. She turned to Colonel Primrose. "Why? I don't mean why did you bring Mrs. Durbin in, but why are you here yourself? What have we got to do with it?"

It was a pleasure to me to see Colonel Primrose even slightly taken aback by a perfectly direct inquiry.

"It's chiefly that you're next door, Mrs. Crane," he answered pleasantly. "And your husband is an old friend of mine. I thought perhaps you'd let me presume on that."

It seemed to me there were four small separate wells of silence receiving those words . . . "Mrs. Crane" and "your husband," . . . and that Colonel Primrose had emphasized them ever so slightly. Courtney's face didn't change, it still had its cool petal-like loveliness; but her long dark lashes lowered, I thought, to conceal the spark that flickered an instant in her gray, faintly slanting eyes.

"I'm sorry, Colonel Primrose," Molly said quickly. "I didn't mean I'm not very happy you're here."

Sometimes I think Colonel Primrose is a very wise man and a very kind one. He'd said a simple thing, but it suddenly made Molly the mistress of her own house, and at home in it, which she hadn't been still standing there in the doorway.

She went over to the sofa.

"Sit down, won't you?"

She looked from Colonel Primrose to Inspector Bigges. "All of us will be glad to tell you anything we know."

"Well, that's the whole thing," Colonel Primrose said.

It always worries me when he acts so urbanely. When butter won't melt in his mouth it's a bad sign.

He looked at Cass now. Cass Crane is a very attractive man, tall and rather quiet. His hair is dark and crisp, his eyes a frosty-gray with smile wrinkles around them, and his mouth big and pleasant. At the moment it was hard to see the picture he always brought to my mind, because the half-smile in one corner of his mouth is so much a part of it, and it was noticeably not there now.

"—This is simply because you happen to be next door to where the body was found," Colonel Primrose said. "What time did you get in, Cass?"

"I got here a little after one," Cass said promptly. "I left the Durbins' around twelve, went down town and phoned around to see if I could locate my wife."

He was looking at Colonel Primrose, but it was Molly he was talking to.

"I came out here, thinking I could get in a window. Which I did. I'd been trying to get hold of Fleming because they told me at the Abbotts' he and Molly had left together. I got him from here. He came around and we had a drink and chewed the fat until about three-thirty. He went home, and I went to bed. I didn't hear anything going on outside. I was dead tired."

"And you, Mrs. Crane?" Colonel Primrose asked.

Molly looked at him with a startled expression on her face.

"Oh, I wasn't here. I stayed all night with Mrs. Latham.

45

She wasn't feeling very well and I didn't think she ought to stay alone."

I must say it was a great tribute. I've seen people drop my great-grandmother's Crown Derby teacups without a flicker, I'd thought . . . but I'd never imagined anyone else had given me credit for a pan as dead—I hoped just then—as Sergeant Buck's itself. It almost broke, however, when Colonel Primrose, caught off guard for a moment, glanced at me a little anxiously, almost as if he believed I hadn't told the truth about why Molly had stayed all night.

Courtney Durbin raised one delicate brow slightly. "Do you feel better now, dear?"

"I feel fine, thanks."

I turned to Molly.

"Why don't you tell Colonel Primrose the truth? He'll find it out if he doesn't already know."

Her face flamed scarlet.

"All right. I stayed at Mrs. Latham's because I didn't want to stay here. But I wasn't here, so I didn't hear anything. And I don't know anything about the body next door."

Courtney stifled a yawn with the scarlet tips of her fingers.

Colonel Primrose nodded politely. "And you, Randy?"

"I walked around to Mrs. Latham's with her and Molly. I stayed a few minutes and went home. Then Cass called and I came here. I left about three-thirty, I guess, and went back home again. Cass and I were here from about one-thirty on. The little guy certainly didn't come near this house while I was here. I never heard a sound outside."

Colonel Primrose spoke very deliberately. "You'd swear to that, Lieutenant Fleming?"

I caught my breath. This was something new. It was a ranking officer speaking as such, and Randy couldn't do anything but tell the truth . . . on his honor he could not. The silence in the room showed that I was not the only one thinking that.

"Certainly, sir," Randy said calmly. "I'll swear to every word of it."

The silence that followed again was broken so quickly that I didn't even have time to relax and say, "Thank God—Lilac is wrong." There was a shouting and a mad scramble outside and then on the steps, the screen door was pushed open and Sheila burst in, dragging her leash, her muzzle to the floor, the hair bristling on her shoulders. She came in a little way and back through the hall, all of us staring at her open-mouthed. Her nails scratched on the bare wood floor as she rounded the corner into the back room.

"Mad dog!" a voice shouted outside. "Mad dog!"

Courtney Durbin's scream was high-pitched and terrifying.

46

I jumped to my feet, but Colonel Primrose was ahead of me and thrust me back.

"Don't move—anybody," he said curtly.

Randy and Cass stopped short. He went to the double doorway. Sheila sniffed up and down the floor, in front of the bar and back across to the desk, growling savagely. Then suddenly she sat down on her red haunches and raised her head, and that long, desperately eerie howl came out of her throat, and again.

Colonel Primrose crossed the room, picked up her leash and drew her away. He patted her and brought her to me. The hair on her head was still disordered, and she was still trembling.

"The dog isn't mad," he said quietly. "Go out, Bigges, and tell them so out there. She's muzzled anyway."

He turned to Courtney. "—Will you go too, please, Mrs. Durbin, across the street and explain to the woman whose child we saw take the dog that there's nothing wrong with her?"

"I'll be glad to, Colonel," Courtney said. She got up and followed Inspector Bigges out.

I was talking to Sheila, trying to quiet her, when something in the room made me look up. Colonel Primrose was standing there looking at Cass and Randy, his face as set as theirs, his eyes hardened to snapping black points.

"D. J. Durbin's driver, whose body was found next door this morning, couldn't have staggered ten feet, with that jolt of poison he had in him," he said slowly. "The dog has just told us he was in this house . . . in the hall, by the desk, by the bar over there. It's precisely the way she acted when the dead man, for some reason unknown to me, was on Mrs. Latham's front porch last night."

He turned to Randy Fleming.

"Which of you carried his dead body over next door I don't know. But you snagged your foot on a rusty nail over there, Fleming . . . and you reported to the Army dispensary for a tetanus shot at 10.20 this morning. I'd like to know what you have to say. Either one, or both of you."

I looked silently at Molly. She was sitting there so still that not even the movement of the pulse in her throat showed even faintly.

8

Colonel Primrose looked from Randy Fleming to Cass Crane, and waited. Molly sat beside me as motionless as a living thing can be. The atmosphere of the room was electric with

47

suspended tension. Each of them—Cass, Molly and Randy —seemed a separate magnetic pole, each holding tight within his own field. Then Cass spoke.

"You can count Randy out of this, Colonel."

His voice was perfectly matter-of-fact.

"What he said is true. The little man didn't come while he was here and nothing happened outside while he was here. The little man was here when he came, and he was dead as a door nail. That's why I called him. I . . . had to get that body out of this house. We were going to put him in his car, but we couldn't find it. Then we decided to stow him over in the Park but some people were there, and we had to put him next door in a hurry."

It seemed to me on the face of it about as cold-blooded a recital as I'd heard . . . calling in a friend to help stow away a dead body as if it were a sack of potatoes. I imagine Colonel Primrose, in his grimly urbane way, must have thought so too.

"—You'd better begin at the beginning."

"Right," Cass said.

He spoke unhesitatingly and looked Colonel Primrose coolly in the eye.

"The last time I phoned from down town the line was busy, so I figured Molly was home. I caught a cab and dashed out. The light in the back room was on, but she didn't answer the bell. I was worried, because I knew she wouldn't go away and leave a light on, in case of a blackout. I didn't want to break in the front, so I climbed over the back fence. The kitchen window was open. I crawled in and came upstairs. The fellow was sprawled out on the floor there, in front of the desk. He'd pulled the telephone off—it was sounding away there by his head."

Colonel Primrose's black eyes were fixed on him with concentrated intensity . . . but it seemed to me, in some curious way, that it was Randy Fleming he was really watching. And it was then I first got the impression that in some way I knew nothing of there was a lot more behind all this than I'd realized.

Randy was standing with one elbow on the mantel. His eyes fixed stolidly on the floor and the downward curve of his mouth gave an odd impression of almost acute bitterness.

"I have plenty of reasons for not wanting Durbin's leg man found dead in my house," Cass said coolly. "I explained a few of them to Randy, and he gave me a hand. Those reasons happen to be more important, in my opinion, and to more people, than helping the local gendarmes determine the actual physical spot he passed out on."

Molly Crane moved then. She hadn't been looking at Cass.

48

Her eyes were fixed on him now, the pulse in her throat throbbing visibly again.

"I wonder if I could be excused, Colonel Primrose?"

She got abruptly to her feet.

"Surely."

He watched her curiously as she moved across to the door and upstairs, and turned back to Cass. Randy Fleming stood there motionless, absorbed in whatever it was going on inside himself.

"—The autopsy showed a large amount of nicotine," Colonel Primrose said. "In Scotch whisky. Where did it come from?"

"I couldn't tell you," Cass said. "It was in the decanter on that wash stand effect. I almost took a shot of it myself. I started to pour a drink while I was waiting for Randy, but I saw the stopper wasn't in the decanter. You don't leave good whisky to evaporate. I looked around and found it under the stand. I figured the little man had probably let it roll there. He didn't seem to be in too good shape, so I didn't take any. A friend of mine analyzed it for me this morning."

"What did you do with it?"

"I dumped all but that much down the sink."

I didn't have to look at Randy Fleming. What was slowly and belatedly dawning in my consciousness must have been in his from the minute he'd walked into this house the night before and seen Achille sprawled dead in front of the desk. It wasn't *doubt* of Molly. Whatever brief doubt of her I'd had in that ghastly moment before she came in from the hospital had vanished, and I was ashamed of its ever having been —even that briefly in my mind. It was fear for her. Just the faintest breath of suspicion getting out. . . . Someone saying, "—Oh yes, you know, she was terribly upset when she left the Abbotts' . . . and my dear, isn't it *lucky* it was Achille and not Cass who drank the poisoned whisky over there . . . just think how it would have looked." Wildfire would have been tortoise-slow compared with it. No matter what anybody ever said, or who was proved to have done it —if they could prove anything—there'd always be the residue . . . always somebody to say, "Yes, they hanged so-and-so, but it *was* strange, wasn't it . . . ?"

Having seen Molly bring up that decanter, and seen her twisted but nevertheless wistful smile as she said something about the prodigal's homecoming, Randy knew, as I knew, that there was no poison in the whisky then. When he helped Cass move Achille's body he was trying, nevertheless, to cut the net that was toiling itself around her feet. It wasn't Cass or Cass's reasons that made him do it, and that made him lie —however true the actual words were—to a superior of-

49

ficer. His calling up to find out about Molly at ten minutes past three that morning was of the same piece of cloth.

And it was his mounting anxiety for her that could be drawing the net tighter now, if he only knew it. Colonel Primrose has a perfectly uncanny way of sensing things he has no right to know logically . . . and Randy and I together there in her living room had between us, in our hands, the pieces to make a hangman's noose that it would be hard to save her from. She'd put the whisky in the decanter, going downstairs to do it. She'd told me she was going to be cold-blooded, and not only knew what she was going to do but had already done it. She'd gone to bed without undressing, and she'd slipped out of my house some time before three o'clock, taken the key with her, come back, and pretended she hadn't left. How could she ever prove to anybody who didn't know her that she hadn't slipped out and come over to empty out the damning evidence of what had happened, and return with me as witness she'd gone to bed at twenty minutes to twelve and got up at half-past seven the next morning?

I could see it already across the front pages of the newspapers as clearly as if I held them printed in my hand.

"What was Achille doing here, Cass?" Colonel Primrose asked.

"Your guess is as good as mine, sir."

Cass added deliberately, "—Or it's something I can't discuss at the moment."

Colonel Primrose looked around. Courtney Durbin was coming through the screen door.

"Then suppose you come and see me at my house," he said. "I'll be there at six."

Courtney came on in.

"That poor woman was really scared," she said. "She thinks Achille's ghost is stalking and that's what's wrong with the dog. And you know, it's a funny thing," she added. "Achille was terrified of dogs. And I've never seen one that didn't know it. They could smell it."

Nobody said anything. She looked at Colonel Primrose.

"What shall I tell Mr. Durbin? He was really devoted to Achille."

"I think I'll see him, as a matter of fact," Colonel Primrose said. "Are you going home now?"

She nodded, and smiled at Cass.

"Tell Molly thanks, will you? And you'll bring her to dinner to-morrow night, won't you?"

She turned to me. "Grace? It's awfully spur of the moment. Are you free? Look and call me, will you? I've got some roast beef, if that's a lure. Goodbye, dear."

She came over, leaned down and kissed me lightly on the

cheek. "Don't look so unhappy, darling. Goodbye, Randy."

Colonel Primrose smiled at me from the doorway.

There was a pretty grim silence in the room as Cass followed them out. He came back, stopped at the bottom of the stairs, looked up for an instant, and then went up, taking them two at a time.

"You know, that guy burns me up," Randy said. He sounded like it. "I can't figure him out. If he thinks Durbin's trying to kill him, what does he go on sticking his neck out for?"

"*Durbin?*" I said.

"Sure. You don't suppose this was an accident, do you? Or the little guy was bringing a . . . a loving cup? You know damn well there was nothing but plain Scotch in that decanter before he got here. If the poor little devil had known it was loaded he wouldn't have slung it into himself. That leaves just one guy, as far as I figure."

"On account of Courtney?" I asked, after a minute.

I was glad I was right about one thing. No suspicion of Molly had ever entered his head.

"I don't know," he said. "From where I sit it looks like a lot of people are getting themselves all tied up in the old struggle for power idea. Something's going on. I don't know whether a guy's apter to kill somebody on account of his wife or on account of his bank book. But I'm just a country boy. I can't figure poisoning a guy for any reason except you hate his guts, personally."

He was staring grimly down at the empty fireplace.

"Jeez, I'd like a drink, but Cass says it isn't safe and maybe he's got something."

He stopped abruptly, looking up at the ceiling. Neither of us could help but hear Molly's voice.

"I'm not staying here, Cass. I've told you I'm not."

And Cass breaking in: "You are staying. I've got a job to do——"

"Let's get out of here," Randy said.

I'd already got up and Sheila was straining on her leash. We let the screen door slam behind us.

He didn't say anything till we'd got out the gate.

"I told her she should have married me," he said then.

"Maybe, if you just stay around, she will," I remarked.

He shook his head.

"She's in love with the guy. She never was with me. And he's okay, as a matter of fact. I felt sorry as hell for him last night. He kept sort of going around, looking at her things. If he lets Courtney bitch this thing up . . ."

At the corner he glanced back. The look on his face was so queer that I said, "What's the matter, Randy?"

51

"I . . . guess I'm scared," he said slowly. "In fact, I know I am. Scared as hell."

He stopped. "I'm going back, Grace. I don't know what's going on, but . . ."

He hesitated a moment.

"Look. Make Molly come over and stay with you. She can't stay in that house. If somebody's spraying bug killer around it's easy as hell to get the wrong bug."

"I think you'd better let them alone, myself," I said. "Nothing can happen with the police around, and everybody on the street watching the place for Achille's ghost to walk."

He came along, still looking back. "Maybe that's it now."

I glanced back myself. As I did a mangy black cat jumped up out of the overgrown grass in the corner yard, and sat on the Cranes' steps washing its paw.

"—I do not believe in ghosts, or in black cats either," I said.

We walked along the parkway to P Street for Randy to get a bus. He was still disturbed, and I think if the bus hadn't come while I was still standing there talking to him he would have gone back. But it did, and he was on it and half-way to the bridge when I remembered suddenly that I hadn't told him about Julie Ross's roomers.

9

I'd meant to tell him, of course, that Mr. Louis Skagerlund, né Lons Sondauer, or whatever, was worried about him and had a gun and to look out for him, but it was too late now. As I went on home I wondered more and more . . . particularly whether Cass's idea of some kind of global strategy in all this—I took it it was his—was as far-fetched as it seemed. People used to say Piccadilly Circus was the hub of the universe, and if you stood on the corner by the Café Royal long enough everybody in the world would pass by. Now that Piccadilly Circus is rimmed with bombed-out, boarded-up windows, Washington has pretty much taken over, and it seems one doesn't have to wait long to see the world, in the French sense at least, not pass by but come apparently to stay.

Just in the small group of people that seemed in the last twenty-four hours to have become suddenly concerned with Cass and Molly Crane there was a microcosmic cross-section of this new macrocosm. Until Washington came to be the hub of the universe neither D. J. Durbin nor Achille had been there. Nor had Corinne's economic swami Duleep Singh, nor Julie's roomers Mr. Sondauer-Skagerlund and the immaculate, slightly desiccated Mr. Austin. With the possible exception of Austin they had all come from great distances, at a time when travel wasn't a simple matter of going to a ticket agent and saying, "To-morrow's plane for Washington, U.S.A., please." And each of them was in a sense a mysterious figure—I don't mean to the State Department or the F.B.I., but to the people who'd meet them casually.

Even in the old Washington there were undoubtedly people on secret missions, whose private business no one knew, but it wasn't a commonplace. One never heard, in those dear dead days, of a hostess inviting a society reporter to a party in order to have it not mentioned. You could hunt a long time, now, before you'd find D. J. Durbin's name in the papers. In fact, I've never seen it there, except when he married Courtney. Or Duleep Singh's, though I've met him constantly at dinners and small parties and the Abbotts' in the three months he'd been here. Actually, I was thinking, I knew almost nothing about either of them, except, as Randy had said of Sondauer-Skagerlund, that both were as rich as skunks.

Still, it wasn't inconceivable that however legitimate their present purpose here was they mightn't have an eye out for what Randy had called the struggle for power. After all, it's going on, and one doesn't have to think very far ahead into the post-war world to realize it will be the bitterest struggle known. Cass Crane, flying back from the undeveloped world that's going to be struggled for, could easily have a better insight into why he had a black cross in front of his name than any of us. It seemed funny, however, to have it all mixed up with Molly and Courtney's struggle for Cass and Julie Ross's struggle with her mother-in-law. It didn't seem to make sense. To think of the poor little troglodyte who was afraid of dogs as a first sacrifice on such an altar seemed as curious as D. J. Durbin, terrified of a black cat's crossing his path and still willing—perhaps—to poison his wife's best friend.

However, it was no stranger, any of it, than that I was on my way home to have an impromptu tea for China Relief because that cave dweller of cave dwellers, Horace Blodgett, newt-souled and dry as dust, was furious with his wife because she'd talked out of turn in Mr. Scofield's grocery store.

It wasn't, actually, Corinne Blodgett who was there. As I started up the front steps Lilac came scuttling out of the kitchen door in the area.

"Mis' Grace!"

Her voice was a loud stage whisper.

"Mis' Blodgett's man was here. He say she can't come to no tea for China Relief, so she sen' a check, an' would you come over to her house for dinner tonight. They got some po'k chops. The Colonel, he going to be there.—An' Mis' Courtney, she waitin' in th' sittin' room."

I took the envelope she held out. It had a check in it, made out to me, for China Relief. It was for twenty-five dollars, and countersigned, as all Corinne's checks are, in Horace Blodgett's precise legal hand. I looked at Lilac.

"Did you tell him——"

" 'Deed I didn' tell him," she interrupted. "I say we're sorry she ain' comin'. But I don' think you ought to say you givin' teas when you ain'."

She went back her way, and I went on mine. Then I was aware she'd stopped and was looking at me, trouble in her old eyes, as I put the key in the lock.

"Miss Molly—she stayin' down at that there place?" she asked through the rails.

I nodded. "Mr. Cass is there."

"Ain' no fittin' place for that chil' to stay," she said darkly. "Things goin' on roun' there ain' ought to go on."

I'd let Sheila go. She bounded down the area steps, and Lilac slammed the door behind her, muttering to herself like some familiar spirit.

I knew, as always, that there was no use stopping then and there and going down to try to find out what she meant. It just added to Randy's uneasiness, and the black cat on the Cranes' steps . . . in spite of the fact that I don't believe in black cats any more than I have a perturbed feeling when the shadow of a buzzard falls across my car on a country road. I don't really believe in the buzzard's shadow, though my kids half do because Lilac taught them to when they were babies, and fear has a substratal contagion you can laugh at if you keep your fingers crossed and knock on wood.

I was figuratively doing both as I went inside. Lilac had quite taken the fine edge off the enjoyment I'd ordinarily have had at getting twenty-five dollars out of Horace Blodgett under false pretenses. Horace must, I thought, be definitely slipping, to be caught out twice within twenty-four hours. Still, I couldn't help wondering why Corinne hadn't come, and why Colonel Primrose was going there to eat pork chops that evening . . . whether Horace had invited him or he'd invited himself.

Courtney came to the door of the sitting room.

"Hello, darling. I hope you don't mind my coming. I'm an awful mess."

She went back and flopped down again on the sofa.

"God, I wish I were dead instead of Achille!"

She sat there grinding out her cigarette into the ashtray on the table long after all possible heat had gone out of it.

"Don't be silly," I said. "What's the matter?"

"Every damned thing in the world, if you want to know," she said wearily, without looking up. "I just can't stand it. I simply can't, Grace. And there's no use saying I'm silly and I've got to, because I can't."

There was a desperate matter-of-fact finality about the way she said it that made it futile to try to say anything.

"I just can't stand having that little —— sitting up there as if she owned Cass, lock, stock and barrel. Oh, I wish I hadn't gone over there in the first place!"

She put her head back against the sofa and closed her eyes, her hands lifeless in her lap. The tears were tangled up in her long dark lashes, not enough of them to escape down her cheeks. Her slight elegant body was as motionless as her hands. She still looked lovely. The delicate velvety peach-blow of her skin, the perfect bone structure under it, her dark hair brushed in an almost Japanese pompadour above her unlined forehead, her eyebrows delicately arched over her violet-veined lids, gave her a fragile exotic loveliness that no inner conflict seemed to mar.

Or I'd always thought so. As I looked at her now I wasn't too sure. Unhappiness and discontent do something to the most perfect face. It wasn't only the lost radiance of the last few months. It was more subtle, as if a spark going out had left bitter ashes behind it.

"Well, Courtney," I said patiently.

This wasn't the first of these scenes. I hope I never have to go through with anybody another week like the one that followed Cass's wedding. It was too harrowing. Just the quiet business of her sitting there as she sat now, without a tear and no hysterics, just eaten by agony, getting thinner and more fragile every day, everything simply gone out of her life. . . . It was so devastating that I was almost glad when she started being publicly vocal about it, which heaven knows she more than was.

When she opened her eyes the pupils were so expanded there was no gray left, and when they'd contracted slowly they were still much larger than most people's. They had a starry liquid quality of depth that made them very soft and completely fascinating—even to women who'd rather have had them sharp as pin points. That's what her tongue could be when she chose, thought actually it seldom was. She was too intelligent, except where Molly was concerned.

She sat up and lighted another cigarette.

"It's not only myself I'm thinking about. It's him. He had everything. All he needed was the right kind of a wife, and nothing could have stopped him. And to think, just *think* —that guy sits on the floor and plays a game of checkers, and lets a little dope bat a pair of yellow eyes at him, and marry him, and take him down to a dump on Beall Street to live. I mean, if she was even pretty, or rich, or well connected!"

"But she's an awfully sweet kid, Courtney," I said.

"Oh, of course! So were dozens of others who bored the pants off him. So did Molly—till I was fool enough to make him pay some attention to her!"

"Well, Courtney," I said again. "If you were in love with him, why didn't you marry him yourself. You had time enough to make up your mind, heaven knows."

We'd always got to this point and she'd always sidestepped it. I expected she would again, but she didn't.

"That's what kills me."

She spoke quietly, but so bitterly that I was a little startled.

"We talked about it, and about his career, and that I was the kind of woman he ought to marry. We both knew it. But he needed to have money. *I* knew that. Then the war came along, and he was going off on these long treks in the wilderness, hunting the materials we lost when the Japs got Burma and Malay. He said he was glad he wasn't married, because it wasn't fair to a girl to be alone and he might easily not get back some trip. I thought he meant it. Then Durbin came along, and it all seemed so simple."

"Courtney!" I said. "Are you saying . . ."

I stopped, not sure at all.

"That's the way it was," she went on. "D. J. isn't in love with me. That has nothing to do with it, Grace. He knew I was in love with Cass and Cass with me. It was his idea, not mine. He needed what I could give him, in the way of contacts, and I needed what he could give me. It was a . . . a marriage of convenience, without the marriage, really."

I sat staring at her, trying to understand what in heaven's name she was talking about.

"Oh, don't be naïve and lower-class, Grace! I wasn't bartering my fair white body—that didn't come into it. It's purely a business arrangement. My God, you're acting the way Horace Blodgett acted. I wanted him to draw up the settlement, so I'd be sure I wasn't getting into anything I couldn't get out of. And Horace! It was defiling the sacred precincts of the law. I couldn't do it. He was furious. He drove me out like the money-changers in the temple. And he's never put his foot in my house. He doesn't speak to me unless he can help it. Horace Blodgett . . . who'd turn a legal noose around the throat of a widow or orphan without batting an eye."

"Well, I'm afraid I agree with him, Courtney," I said.

"I don't see that it's anybody's damn business," she said

curtly. "If it's agreeable to D. J. and me, I don't see that it hurts anybody. At least there's no pretense to it, and there are lots of duration marriages you can't say that for. I don't believe being level-headed is indecent and being hysterical is romantic. I'll admit I figured the war would be over sooner than it looks like it's going to be."

"And . . . then you were going to marry Cass?"

She nodded slowly.

"Everything would have been wonderful, then."

"—And Cass went back on the bargain."

She didn't say anything for a moment.

"No. He didn't know. I was a fool not to tell him. I was going to, and then I didn't like to, some way. Then when Horace Blodgett took on the way he did—and I don't know anybody who has more respect for money—I thought I was wise not to. And . . . I thought Cass knew. When I told him I was going to marry D. J. he didn't say anything for a few minutes, and then he said, 'How long do you think it's going to last?' He was being sardonic, I knew, but I thought the way he looked at me that he knew, underneath. When he said, 'Well, I guess you've got what you want,' I thought he *couldn't* think that, not really. Not as well as he knew me."

It sounded rather like straining at a gnat, I thought. The camel still gagged me.

"People don't know D. J. really," she said, after a moment. "His accident makes him shy and reserved. The bones didn't knit properly after he broke his hip. People say he's ruthless, but he's been charming to me."

"It would be nice," I said. "if you'd fall in love with him, and really marry him, darling."

She shook her head quickly. "He has a cruel streak too. I see that with other people. That little Achille, who'd have cut off his right hand for him."

She got up, went to the window and stood looking out for an instant.

"The only thing that worries me a little is that he . . . might fall in love with me," she said. "That terrifies me. As Horace said, there's no court that would uphold the kind of contract we have. I ought to have been more business-like, not less."

She gave a violent start suddenly, her face turning as pale as her dress. It was nothing but Sheila, banging open the door from the basement and bursting into the room.

"Sorry!" she said.

She was trembling a little even then.

"I'm jittery. Make me an old-fashioned, will you? I've got to have something to steady my nerves before I go back. I'm

57

really a mess. I just don't know what to do, Grace! I'm so frightened I'm beside myself. It's everything . . . everything in my life has gone to hell!"

She stood there trying to get hold of herself while I made the old-fashioned.

"Here you are," I said.

Her hands were shaking as she took it, and she lowered her eyes to keep from meeting mine.

"What's *really* the matter, Courtney?" I asked. "Besides Cass."

She started to say something and changed her mind.

"Not knowing about little Achille," she said then, slowly. "I don't know whether somebody thought they could get at D. J. through him, or whether. . . . Oh, I just don't know. I don't dare think about it."

She closed her eyes for an instant.

"I don't dare," she repeated. "—Some queer people come to see D. J. I've wondered if they and all the others that come know he has a recording system so everything they say is down in their own voices. He keeps the records locked. He doesn't trust a secretary to take them off. He doesn't trust anybody. Oh, well . . ."

She put her glass down.

"I feel better. I'd better go . . . Colonel Primrose was talking to him, and they ought to be through by now. Oh, Grace, you don't know how I wish I'd never got mixed up with *any* of it! I guess Horace Blodgett was right."

"I wouldn't be surprised," I said.

10

The only surprising thing, in fact, was that she would have gone to him about it originally, I thought as I went up to take a shower and dress. It showed the same blind spot in her makeup that thinking Cass Crane would accept the cold crumbs from D. J. Durbin's table showed, and her failure to see that Molly Crane had something she definitely lacked. Still, it was bitter bread she was eating . . . too bitter to go on swallowing for long, now that the only thing that had made it palatable in the first place was gone.

I've never been able to decide whether Courtney Durbin was extraordinarily complex or just a simple child of nature, and I still wasn't able to. She could be a perfect fiend, as she'd been to Molly at the Abbotts' the night before, or as warm and generous as I knew she'd been to Julie Ross. I'd seen her in a kind of anguish talking about Cass Crane, and

58

cold-bloodedly mercenary as indicated by her arrangements with Mr. Durbin. Which was her dominant self I simply couldn't say. And above all why she went to Horace Blodgett with any such bizarre and opportunist scheme—to call it the least offensive names I can think of—I had no idea. Sitting next to him at his dinner table two hours later I was still more astonished that she should have so mis-estimated him.

But before that a very curious thing happened. At least it seemed curious to me, happening when it did and where it did.

I came downstairs to go out to get a bus over to the Blodgetts'. I wasn't sure whether it was going to come actually under the head of pleasure-driving or not. Colonel Primrose hadn't phoned, and Horace Blodgett expects his guests to be on time. Like many other Washingtonians I've never had time entirely to figure out the bus system's riddle, and I'd rather walk than transfer to some uncharted line from the one I knew. The streets are less crowded too.

As I started out Lilac came out of the sitting room.

"Mis' Courtney mus' lef' this," she said. "I don' know if it's gold but we ain' want nobody say it was stole in our house."

She handed me a chamois skin case. In it was a gold cigarette box with a quite lovely and elaborate clasp of baguette diamonds and emeralds. I put it back in the case and put it in my bag.

"I'll take it by to her," I said. It was a rather more valuable bauble than I liked lying loose around the house, even though I'm not as suspicious of people as Lilac is. I had to go past the Durbins' to get to the Blodgetts' anyway.

I got off the bus at 21st Street and walked over to Massachusetts Avenue. The Durbins have a large and imposing mansion with a high wrought-iron fence around it above 24th Street. A messenger boy was just leaning his bicycle against the fence as I got there. He took a box out of the wire basket on the handlebars and yanked at the gate, not knowing that it was kept locked and he had to pull the bell at the side.

"There's a bell," I said. I came up and pointed to it.

He pulled it and we stood there waiting until the mechanism clicked. We went in. The butler opened the front door about as automatically as we reached the top step.

"Is Mrs. Durbin in?" I asked.

"Yes, Madam. Madam is on the terrace. If Madam will excuse me, please . . ."

He turned to the messenger boy to take the box.

"—Ah ah!" the boy said. "It's for Mr. D. J. Durbin. It's valuable. I got to put it in his own hands personally.—Cripes, limber up. It ain't a bomb. Where's the ol' massa

59

himself? I got my instructions straight from the Ambassador."

He winked at me.

"Always gets 'em—try it some time," he whispered as we followed Flowers . . . which, believe it or not, really was the Durbins' colored butler's name. I'd known him when he called people Miss and Ma'am, before he learned how the other half lives.

Courtney and D. J. Durbin were on the terrace outside the library windows. I saw them before I saw they had guests, and also before I saw the guests were Mr. Sondauer-Skagerlund and his friend, the cool and sharp-eyed Mr. Austin. And brief as the space from the French windows down to the flagstones was, I caught the sharp interchange of glances that took place. Mr. Durbin's angry accusing flash at Courtney, the two men's, surprised, at each other, both of them questioningly at their host. Even Courtney looked a little amazed. I gathered that it was an extremely private party, and that Flowers had been as deceived by my dinner dress as by the messenger boy's Ambassador. It shot through my mind to tell the boy to try that some time.

"Darling!"

Courtney came forward, her hand out.

"—It's to-morrow, not to-night," she whispered quickly.

"I just dropped in to return this, angel," I said, and handed her the cigarette case.

Then my heart took a sudden nose-dive down to my stomach. She'd gone as white as the painted iron table behind her. Mr. Durbin's liquid dark eyes were instantly alert and alive as burning coals. I'd made a mistake. I knew that, without any idea of anything I could say to try to cover it up. It would have been worse, no doubt, if I'd tried, because he'd already seen her hand tremble as she reached out to take it.

"Thanks," she said.

I never heard the word said with greater irony, in effect if not in sound.

It happened very quickly, the surface was as quickly smooth. Mr. Durbin bowed to me and smiled.

"Have you met our friends? Mr. Skagerlund, Mrs. Latham. And Mr. Austin."

He couldn't have spoken more pleasantly. And this was funny too . . . for neither Mr. Skagerlund nor Mr. Austin wanted D. J. Durbin to know we'd met, or at least where we'd met. If they'd written it in scarlet letters on the side of the house they couldn't have got it across to me with more clarity. It was in every drop of his essential juices standing like dewy pearls on Mr. Sondauer-Skagerlund's brow. And a few were on Mr. Austin's.

"Yes, we've met," I said, smiling as sweet as honey from

the honeycomb. "At Cass Crane's, Wednesday night. You don't remember me, I'm afraid."

If they could all make Courtney uncomfortable, I thought, it seemed only reasonable for them to do a little intensive perspiring themselves. Which they were indeed doing. I saw D. J. Durbin's eyes narrow like a cat's for just an instant, before he turned to Courtney. She'd put her hand lightly on the messenger boy's shoulder and was waiting for her husband to turn around.

"This lad has a package for you, D. J.," she said. "Do you want me to sign for it?"

She spoke to me in an undertone as she signed his name to the boy's receipt. "—Wait, Grace . . . I'll go to the door with you."

I saw Mr. Durbin weighing the package in his mind as he put it on the table by the cocktail tray. It was about as big as a shoe box. In fact, it was a shoe box, and loosely wrapped, so that he pulled the cord off with a turn of his hand and brushed the paper aside. He flipped the lid off.

A tiny black kitten, so small its fur had not really grown yet, raised its head and mewed. And then the most dreadful thing happened. If that kitten had been a rattlesnake coiled to strike, or some unspeakably loathsome thing, the effect on D. J. Durbin could not have been so awful. He lurched back with a horrible cry, his face white and contorted with terror, and raised his stick and smashed it down on the table. The glasses crashed right and left, and the kitten, missed by inches, its instinct asserting itself without any knowledge of evil, sprang out of the box and off the table, its shaky legs hardly strong enough to carry it. Mr. Durbin whipped up his stick again, his face like a madman's.

"Oh, don't, don't!" Courtney cried.

She darted forward and reached down for the kitten, and Durbin's stick came down, before he could stop it, almost with full force, across her hands.

She managed to push the little beast over toward me.

"Get it, Grace! Get it and go, quickly!"

The two guests were standing there as if paralyzed. I was only conscious of one thing—that I wanted to be somewhere else, right away. I bent down, scooped up the kitten, and just ran.

The messenger boy ran with me, and we got through the house and outside the front door, and stood staring at each other. His face was a little white, and I know mine was more than a little.

"Well . . . jeez," he said. He put his hand out and touched the kitten. "—I guess he don't like cats."

I got back part of my breath.

"It's a black cat," I said.

"Yeah, I know." He shook his head. "I could take it," he said, tentatively. "I got a kid sister, and my mother's nuts about cats."

I handed it to him quickly. "Take it, then . . . and get it away from here."

As we got to the gate I glanced back.

"I wouldn't go back there, lady," he said seriously. "You and me weren't very popular, if you noticed."

"I guess you're right," I said, trying to smile. "Well, goodbye, and take care of it, won't you?"

We waved back at each other after I'd crossed the street, and I pulled myself together, or as much as I could, and hurried on to the Blodgetts'.

11

Corinne Blodgett came out into the hall to greet me. She was swathed in one of those indefinite things of hers that has no beginning or end, if a lot of middle, and while not, apparently, sewed together any place, has never to my knowledge come apart in public. This one was a lot of misty blue-rose-gray chiffon that made her look rather like an ambulatory cloud with a solid center.

"He didn't mean to be unkind, dear," she whispered, kissing my cheek. "He insisted on sending the check. But let's not talk about it, shall we?"

The effect of the day's strain was still visible on her face, however. It wasn't as fresh and rosy-pink and white as it usually was, and her blue eyes weren't as childlike and gay, or when they were there was effort behind them. It might, of course, have been the heat and the street car, I thought, as much as Horace. I learned later that actually it was the anniversary of her daughter's death . . . which shows why no less a person than Sherlock Holmes once pointed out you can't judge any woman by ordinary norms.

She raised her voice to its normal pitch.

"Come along, Grace. Horace has already looked at his watch twice, my dear."

She led me through to where Horace Blodgett was at that moment looking at his watch for at least the third time. It seemed odd to be having cocktails in his library, but kind of him to allow it, as it's air-conditioned and the rest of the house isn't.

"I'm sorry I'm late, Horace," I said.

I wasn't sure, with the new picture I'd got of him as domestic ogre and disperser of the money-changers, whether he'd spring at me with a leather thong or just send me home dinnerless. But he was just the same as he's always been—dry and unflurried, parchment—or was it papyrus—garbed in wool white linen, taking off his rimless pince nez with his thumb and forefinger and snapping the cord up under his lapel as he put them in his breast pocket, before he held out his hand to me.

"Good evening, my dear." He wouldn't say I wasn't late, because I was—six minutes by the clock in the corner. "Will you have a cocktail? A client sent me a case of champagne. It needs the bitters as disguise—otherwise I shouldn't desecrate it."

He raised his glass.

"It's a pleasure to have our friends with us this evening."

I'd already nodded to Colonel Primrose and, a little to my surprise, Swami Duleep Singh, who were standing together near the fireplace. Above them was the portrait of the Blodgetts' daughter, done the year she came out by a painter who'd caught her extraordinary vivid quality unmarred by the then mode. Her brilliant hair was done up sort of Romney-flamboyant, and she wore a simple square-necked white frock, as if the artist had wanted to avoid the styles of those fabulous pre-'29 days ever becoming comical and detracting from the eternal loveliness of his subject.

When I'd thought the strain of Corinne's day was still visible on her face, I'd forgot the strain of my last few moments, and its probable effect on mine. I had, that is, until I saw Colonel Primrose's black eyes sharpen and the smile of his face become static for an instant as he looked at me . . . the cobbler sticking to his last, in season and out. I dare say there was effort behind the smile in my childlike eyes too, just then, as I realized I'd arrived breathless and still fairly goggle-eyed.

"This dear child was practically running, Horace," Corinne said. "You don't realize, my dear, that while the street car company is gracious enough to let you ride a whole week for a dollar and a quarter, they can't have equipment precisely where you want it the minute you want it."

"Yes, my dear," Horace said with domestic amiability. He smiled dryly at me and filled my glass again.

"I should think, Colonel, wouldn't you, that even Horace would have to relax a few of his rules, in deference to the larger effort? I sometimes think his dear mother must have swaddled him in a strait jacket. Are you so determinedly punctual in your country, Mr. Singh? Perhaps you can explain to my husband some time about nirvana."

"It is mañana you mean, my dear," Horace said.

"Well, whatever it *is*," Corinne said. "It's something you ought really to learn, Horace."

He shook his head. "It's my experience that if you put off

63

doing things, and don't do them punctually, the chance to do them well passes. You're likely to bungle, and be caught in the mesh of circumstance. You've seen that in your country, Mr. Singh? And you in your business . . . or is it profession, John?"

He looked at Colonel Primrose.

"Yes. I think I could give you instances, military and private."

The man announced dinner.

"It's certainly true of pork chops, I'll have to admit," Corinne said, putting down her glass and getting up. "I would have had fried chicken, but Horace said the last chickens we've had tasted like sea gulls. Though I've never seen why sea gulls shouldn't be very good to eat. They're very pretty when they fly."

I've always known that Colonel Primrose has X-ray eyes, but perhaps he's a swami too. Both he and Duleep Singh were apparently equally aware that there was a dark man in my immediate past. It was so much in their glances every time I met them that at the advent of the squash I decided I'd relieve their minds.

"I had the most extraordinary experience on the way here," I said. "It was why I was late, Horace. I stopped to take Courtney her cigarette case. Somebody had sent Mr. Durbin a black kitten. It seems he doesn't like black cats or kittens. He was considerably unstrung."

"Well, that's very silly," Corinne said. "I don't possibly see how a black cat can be regarded as bad luck. Horace, you *must* eat your squash. Do you, Colonel Primrose?"

He was looking at me thoughtfully.

"Cats interest me very much," he said. "I've heard of people who were really deathly afraid of them. Let's see . . . it's called aelurophobia. A morbid or pathological fear of cats. There's a kindred obsession known as galeanthropy, the mental delusion that one has actually become a cat. I've never run into that myself."

"The other is fairly common," Horace Blodgett said, "in non-pathological forms. Shakespeare has something about it. 'Some men there are love not a gaping pig, some that are mad if they behold a cat.' I've only known one person in my life who had it to a marked degree. That was———"

"That was a long time ago and in another country, Horace," Corinne said.

"I'm sorry, my dear."

He turned to Colonel Primrose with a dry chuckle.

"Why anyone should send Durbin a black kitten. . . . If they'd sent him a black puma it would be understandable."

Colonel Primrose smiled without saying anything. It seemed to me he was taking all this rather more seriously than I, certainly, had meant it to be. Otherwise I'd have mentioned Courtney's getting in the way of the stick. I was carefully avoiding that, however, for a number of reasons, chiefly because I knew she'd want me to.

"It was an unbelievable performance, really," I said. "Most people who wish on stars don't claim it's serious. But there was no disguise about this. I was just about paralyzed, and Mr. Sondauer-Skagerlund——"

If I had dropped a polite bombshell deliberately into the middle of the table, the effect could not have been more definite, though actually quite urbane.

The three men, their forks at varying stages to their mouths, let them rest motionless for a perceptible instant.

Colonel Primrose said, "Who did you say, Mrs. Latham?"

"A guest at the Durbins'," I said. "He's introduced as Mr. Skagerlund, but Randy Fleming says his name's Sondauer. Lons Sondauer."

Duleep Singh put down his fork and picked up his water glass, but not before he had looked at Horace Blodgett, who in turn looked at Colonel Primrose. When Horace turned to me there was nothing in his voice to indicate that it was a matter of any importance.

"Was he the only guest?"

"A Mr. Austin was there."

No glances were exchanged, but the effect was the same.

"Had you met them before, Mrs. Latham?" Colonel Primrose asked.

"They came to see Cass Crane the night he got back," I answered. "Randy and I were waiting for Molly."

"You're quite sure—or Fleming was—that the name was Sondauer?"

"There's no doubt of it, I imagine. He'd signed Randy's short snorter bill. And his landlady heard him and Austin talking about Randy."

"His landlady?"

It was the first time Duleep Singh had spoken.

"Julie Ross," I said. "They're staying with her."

Horace Blodgett put his napkin on the table and pushed his chair back.

"My dear, will you excuse us, please?"

Both Colonel Primrose and Duleep Singh got up at precisely the same moment.

Corinne said, "Certainly, my dear," and turned to me as the library door closed. "I don't know, my dear," she said. "Either Horace has something definitely in his mind, or he's going to the most bizarre lengths to avoid eating his yellow vegetables."

But it wasn't the squash. That was apparent when the library door was finally opened again.

"I think you had better let me look into this," Horace was saying as Corinne and I went in. "It's a legal——"

He stopped and moved the papers on his desk so the man could put down the coffee tray.

It was curious how they drank their coffee and Duleep Singh had a second cup while Horace and Colonel Primrose went through the elaborate ritual of a teaspoonful of brandy in glasses big enough for goldfish bowls. Time, seemingly of the essence, seemed also to make no difference. I had a feeling, nevertheless, largely the product of my long association with Colonel Primrose, that Lady Macbeth's ghost was going to materialize in the door and say, "Stand not upon the order of your going, but go at once." And Horace put down his glass and rose.

"My dear, I am going over to the Durbins' for a few minutes. Perhaps a rubber of bridge . . ."

The other men got up, Colonel Primrose glancing at the clock in the corner.

"I have a little business with Mr. Durbin, at ten o'clock," he said. "I think I'll go along too."

"I had best come too, as this is largely my problem," Duleep Singh said. He bowed over Corinne's hand, bowed to me and moved to the door before either of them. "—It might be wise to call Mr. Crane, at this point?" he asked quietly.

Horace looked at him thoughtfully for an instant.

"I think it would.—My dear, will you show Mr. Singh the telephone upstairs? We will wait here."

As soon as they were gone he turned to Colonel Primrose.

"May I ask what your business with Mr. Durbin is? I ask it in the interest of my client."

Colonel Primrose hesitated for only an instant.

"I see no reason why I shouldn't tell you. Inspector Bigges is meeting me there at ten o'clock. Durbin will, in all probability, be put under arrest."

Horace Blodgett's dry tones never seemed to change. "And . . . charged?" he asked.

"And charged with the killing of Achille, and the attempted murder of Cass Crane," Colonel Primrose said.

He turned to me.

"I'm not sure this particular black kitten wasn't an evil omen in fact, as well as in superstition," he said. He hesitated again. "I hope it didn't cross Courtney's path?"

Colonel Primrose turned back to Horace.

"If Corinne won't object, I'd like to take Mrs. Latham," he said. "Courtney might . . . like to have someone there."

"Corinne won't mind," Horace said.

In the hall he got Colonel Primrose's hat from the closet and put Duleep Singh's on the table.

"I'd like to get there before those people leave. Singh can follow us."

He looked at his watch. "It's twenty past nine. They'll probably just be getting up from the table."

I shook my head, mentally, as we went down the steps, thinking that on the contrary they'd probably been up a considerable time. The look D. J. Durbin had given his guests and their obvious discomfiture at my mention of their apparently off-the-record visit to Cass Crane's, plus the affair of the black kitten, didn't add up in my mind to anything that presaged a pleasant social evening. Even presuming that Courtney had got them through the roast—also presuming, of course, that she really had one—I couldn't quite see the three gentlemen lingering over port and cigars and telling stories, unless possibly sad stories of the deaths of kings.

It took us about five minutes to walk there. No one said anything, each occupied with what must have been highly individual cargoes of thought, of varying weights and sources. And it must have taken another five minutes, though it seemed much longer that we stood outside the wrought-iron gate ringing the bell, for Flowers' reluctant figure to appear in the door. It was really reluctant, too.

He recognized the three of us simultaneously as he came down the steps.

"I'm very sorry, Colonel, sir, Mr. Blodgett, sir, and Madam," he said.

It was like interviewing a prisoner behind the bars, though which side was which I didn't know, for Flowers has a profound dignity matching his position and his diction, both of which are genuinely impressive. The sound of his diction especially. If the words he uses don't always actually mean what he uses them to mean, it's beside the point, for they convey his meaning perfectly.

"I'm very regrettable indeed, sir," he said, "but it's indispensable. My instructions are to give admission to no one. That's my instructions, with full signification."

He looked at me.

"It's the result of my original error. The offence is not

personable, sir. I was instructed that if the Old Man himself rung the bell I was to tell him to return to his habitation."

I doubt if either Colonel Primrose or Horace Blodgett had ever before in all his life been told he could go to hell with quite so much dignity. And we were still on the wrong side of the iron gate. Colonel Primrose glanced at his watch. In a short time an open sesame would arrive in the form of Inspector Bigges. Until then, I supposed, there wasn't much to do.

"Is Mrs. Durbin in, Flowers?" he asked.

"Madam is in retirement in her room, sir."

At that moment, however, madam became visible through the open door, just reaching the bottom of the elaborate curving staircase. I saw she had retired, however; she had on an ivory lace negligee and ivory kid slippers. As I glanced quickly at her hand on the stair rail I saw it was bandaged, and so was the other hanging at her side.

She came across the hall to the door. As she saw us I thought there was a definite tone of relief in her voice. "—Oh, hello—come in, please."

She put her hand out, the mechanism clicked in the gate lock.

"I beg your pardon, Madam," Flowers said. "My instructions——"

"These are my instructions," Courtney said shortly. "Come in—please. I'm sorry. I'm sure if Mr. Durbin had known . . ."

She looked at Horace Blodgett and smiled. "I'm sorry your first visit should be . . . obstructed."

She led the way into the drawing room at the left of the wide hallway, glancing at the closed door of the library balancing it on the right. There was something very curious in her expression. I saw Colonel Primrose glance at her bandaged hands, but it was her face that his black eyes were fixed on, with no attempt to conceal either his interest or his concern. It had a substratum of pallor and intensity that all her poise couldn't have disguised if she'd been trying to. It wasn't only pain and shock, or chiefly that. It was plain downright cold and bitter fury. Her eyes looked the way dry ice feels when you touch it.

"Sit down, will you?" she said. "I'm very glad you all came. I was just packing some things to leave."

Her voice as she said that was as cool and controlled as I've ever heard it. She looked at Horace.

"You were . . . quite right, Mr. Blodgett. I should have taken your advice in the beginning. You can pay too high a price—even for money."

I suppose Horace Blodgett could have been called gentle,

for a moment, if you could scrape through the dry leaves of his voice and manner and find what was underneath.

"I was a little severe, perhaps. A lawyer doesn't like to see the law made a mockery of. However, Mrs. Durbin, I didn't come because I feel any less strongly about it now than I did then. I am here entirely on business. I would like to see Mr. Durbin."

I don't know whether Courtney thought I'd told Colonel Primrose and Horace about her earlier visit to me and my late visit to her, and thought their pure chivalry had brought them. She looked a little startled.

"—I didn't know you did business with my husband."

"My clients do, however."

He glanced across the hall at the library door, looking at his watch. His clients, insofar as Duleep Singh represented them, hadn't appeared. Duleep Singh must have been having a longer chat with Cass Crane than he had planned, I thought, or perhaps Corinne had got him into some esoteric corner and he was too much of a gentleman to cut and run.

"He's in the library, with Mr. Skagerlund and Mr. Austin," Courtney said. "Perhaps you know them?"

There was a frail desiccated ghost of some curious expression behind Horace's pince nez before he removed them and slipped them into his pocket.

"I . . . might," he said. "At any rate, I shall intrude upon them . . . with your permission."

The sound that came from Courtney's lips could possibly be called the crust of a laugh. It was certainly hollow.

"For whatever it is worth, Mr. Blodgett, you have my permission—with pleasure. I don't advise you to do it. The atmosphere is likely to be . . . explosive."

"I will risk it," Horace said equably.

He turned to Colonel Primrose.

"If Singh comes, John, keep him in here, please, until I have a chance to talk things over. I am uniquely interested in Mr. . . . Skagerlund."

He looked at me with his dry smile . . . still not believing, I realized, that Randy and I knew what we were talking about. At this stage my own curiosity about Mr. Sondauer-Skagerlund was beyond the point of being unique. It was practically dithering. But Colonel Primrose, with his methodical first-things-first approach, was interested in Courtney. Even when he was nodding assent to Horace he had the tail of his eye fixed on her. It was an involved and complex tail at that. I couldn't even guess what was going on in his mind behind it.

We were sitting, he and I, on a summer-muslin covered sofa pulled out at an oblique angle from the ornate fireplace, so that we had a full view of the library door. Horace Blodgett reached it, and put his hand out to the silver knob. Knowing him as a civilized social entity, I expected, naturally, to see him knock, and wait until he was asked either to come in or to stay out. Instead, he calmly opened the door and started in. Or rather, he just started. It was as if some invisible hand had held him there, motionless, on the threshold, for an instant, before he went on in and closed the door quietly behind him.

I looked at Colonel Primrose with an only half-suppressed smile. Mr. Skagerlund apparently *was* Mr. Sondauer, then, no matter who Mr. Sondaeur might be, and it was a matter of mild pleasure to me to see Horace Blodgett, who in his career must have had many rabbits pulled out of legal hats at him, being surprised at this one he'd been prepared for in advance. Then it occurred to me suddenly that maybe it was the clean one, as Julie Ross had called the impeccable Mr. Austin, who was the shock. If the one could change his name, there was no reason the other couldn't.

It was still Courtney Durbin that Colonel Primrose was interested in.

"What did you do to your hands, Courtney?"

She glanced quickly at me. "Hasn't Grace told you?"

I shook my head . . . feeling the tail of the Colonel's eye resting on me then.

"Mr. Durbin was thrashing his stick at a poor little black kitten some ass sent him, and he hit me instead."

She looked at her hands.

"The maid taped them for me. I'll have to have them X-rayed in the morning. They're rather painful."

"You should have done it this evening," Colonel Primrose said gravely. "Why——"

The color showed in her cheeks, and her face hardened a little.

"D. J. was very firm about my not leaving the house and not having a doctor in," she said quietly. "I . . . it hurt so much when it happened that I couldn't think clearly enough to know what I was doing. It's only been about the last half hour that I've been able to make any decision that involved . . . doing anything at all."

"I'm sorry," Colonel Primrose said.

"You needn't be. I deserve anything I get."

She spoke evenly, looking at her hands again.

"Mr. Blodgett told me that in the beginning.—You've heard about spiritual pain, but it doesn't mean very much, not until you've felt it. You think you can take a chance on it that you'd never think of taking on being physically hurt. But I don't know, now."

She looked at her hands and shook her head. "It's nothing to the kind of pain you can have in your heart. But we never know that until it's too late."

I couldn't tell whether Colonel Primrose knew what she was talking about or not. Horace may have told him what she'd told me, because they're old friends. Not many people I know except his Army friends call him by his first name. He was acting now, of course, as if he had the whole background, which meant nothing. If Colonel Primrose had got lost in a vacuum he'd have proceeded as if nature, not he, abhorred it, and he was very much at home.

"Who sent the kitten?" he asked.

"I don't know," Courtney said shortly. "If D. J. does, he didn't say. It isn't the first time. I don't mean he was sent one before, or he wouldn't have opened that package. But one was in his car out in front one day, and he nearly went into spasms. He smashed the window glass and almost killed poor Achille. He did kill the kitten."

"It was black, too?" Colonel Primrose asked quietly.

She nodded.

"He seems to have the most unbelievable superstitious fear of them. It juts doesn't make sense in a man who hasn't fear or respect for God, man or the devil. Unless he thinks a black cat *is* the devil."

She looked across the hall. It was the first time she'd really showed any of the nervous tension she was under. Before, when she'd looked across toward the library door, it was as if she were waiting for the atmosphere to explode. Now it seemed as if she were disturbed and even frightened, perhaps, because it hadn't. I remember thinking it was true that women frequently don't realize a man may behave differently in business and in social contacts, if that observation doesn't sound too much as if I were plagiarizing Miss Dix.

"—It doesn't extend to any other——?"

Colonel Primrose never finished that question. The door of the library opened, and Horace Blodgett came out. Or stopped in the doorway, actually, looking across the hall toward us.

"I think you had better come here, John," he said.

There was a fraction of an instant when nobody moved.

Sitting there half-paralyzed with a kind of instant intuitive apprehension that something, I didn't know what, must have happened, it flashed into my mind suddenly and incongruously that if it had, Horace Blodgett was then and there being one of the best reasons for the dusty-dry type of lawyer and friend. There was no fuss or emotion. He simply stood there, making that statement quite in his usual tone of voice.

In his hand he held a sheaf of papers with a blue cover folded the way legal papers are.

It was only for a fraction of an instant that we sat there. Colonel Primrose was up and across the room much faster than he normally moves. I saw a sharp spasm of pain shoot across Courtney's face, and realized that her hands had contracted suddenly on the arms of her chair. Otherwise she sat motionless. Colonel Primrose reached the door, and stopped, just as Horace had stopped when I'd thought he had recognized Mr. Skagerlund—or Mr. Austin. He stood there on the threshold, his head turning slowly from side to side. I knew perfectly well even from where I was that his sparkling black eyes were moving with the precision of a camera lens from one object in the room to another, photographing it all in his mind. And I knew too that something had happened.

Courtney Durbin's body moved in a futile effort to raise itself from the chair.

"I . . . must go," she said. "He must be . . . he's probably had a stroke . . ."

It may be unkind and macabre to say it, but if I've ever heard wishful thinking expressed out loud I heard it then.

She leaned forward and managed to get up. I followed her across the room. She moved more steadily and quickly than I'd thought she'd be able to.

We were half-way across the hall before Colonel Primrose, still standing there, turned and saw us.

"—Don't, Courtney," he said quietly. "Go back and sit down. It's . . . too late."

She stood rigidly still for an instant, then ran forward too quickly for him to stop her. In the doorway her hand went slowly up to her throat and she took a step back, swaying a little. Colonel Primrose motioned sharply to me. I ran up and caught hold of her, trying to steady her shaking body.

He went inside and closed the door. She clung to me for an instant, still shaking. Then suddenly her body went taut, her head snapped up, and she stood there looking at me, her face an extraordinary pattern of shifting emotions.

"—Oh, quick, Grace!" she whispered then. "Quick!"

It was one of the most agonized sounds I've ever heard come from anyone, and her face was as tortured as the sound.

"Oh, my God, *quick!*"

13

She shook off my hands and ran past the staircase toward the back of the house. I followed her without any idea of what it was about, except that it was so desperately urgent that in all the world nothing else mattered for her just then.

She pushed open the door of a room behind the library and switched on the light. I heard a muted whirring, of the sort a phonograph needle makes on a record before the music begins, and then I remembered what she'd told me this afternoon.

There was a large mahogany chest of drawers standing against what would be the library wall, a bust of Voltaire sitting on top of it. That cynical fascinating leer of his was fixed on us, the bronze high-lighted so that he looked alive, as if it were us he meant to be grinning at across the span of two centuries . . . and when Courtney seized him and thrust him into my hands he grinned up at me until I turned him over.

She ripped off the gold brocade he'd been sitting on and released a spring at either end of the top drawer. The top and front of the chest moved up and back, folding against the wall, and left a recording machine in front of us, the mechanism quietly revolving away. It was an automatic arrangement, one arm at that instant in the act of very intelligently shifting a black record under the needle. She raised the arm and lifted off the three top records, and then, as if she couldn't be sure, took the fourth. She put the needle gently down on the fresh disc, put the top down and the brocade back in place. When she took the Voltaire from me I suppose his expression hadn't really changed, but it seemed to me his grin was a little more cynical, and I reached up and moved his face around so he'd look at the floor instead of me.

"Come on," she whispered quickly.

We got back into the drawing room. She stood there with the records in her hand, hesitating, glanced across the hall and went quickly to the end of the room. Against the wall in the angle of the windows at the front and side of the house was a handsome Chippendale phonograph cabinet. She lifted the lid, took off the record that was on the turntable, slipped the four discs onto it and put the other back on top. She turned around, leaving it open, came back and sank down in her chair again. Her face was so white it was almost green. She let her hands rest in her lap and closed her eyes. I could almost feel the waves of mental relief and of re-

73

turning physical pain that went through her. She opened her eyes again, and pressed her wrists together tightly, as if to relieve the pain in her hands.

"I don't think you're being very wise, Courtney," I said, uneasily. "You can get yourself in a lot of trouble . . ."

"It doesn't matter," she said.

Then she stared at me, doubt sharpening suddenly to fear, as if the fact that my position in all this might be very different from her own had just that instant flashed into her mind.

"Grace, you won't tell him! There's nothing else I could do . . . believe me, nothing!"

It would be foolish for me to attempt to say I'd never tried to help conceal evidence from Colonel Primrose before, nor do I know why the idea should have bothered me then. But it did. I was very uneasy about it. Doing something on the impulse of the moment was one thing. This seemed to me rather different.

"He's bound to find out about it," I said uncertainly. "He always does."

"Then let him," she said. "But Grace, you've got to believe me, there's——"

The doorbell buzzed urgently somewhere in the silent reaches of the big house. Courtney sat abruptly erect, listening, her lips parted, the pupils of her eyes distended, her breath coming in quick gasps—in the space of a fraction of a second as near sheer panic as I've ever seen anyone in my life. If Colonel Primrose had come in then. . . . But he didn't. He went down the hall from the library to the front door, glancing across at me and shaking his head soberly—telling me, in effect, I supposed, that he was as bewildered about the whole business as I was.

A clock somewhere struck ten. Ten slow softly booming notes can take a long time striking. We sat there listening to them as she relaxed slowly back into her chair, listening to them and to the subdued voices of the men at the door, and to the changing quality of sound as their feet moved from the stone steps outside to the polished hardwood of the hall. The clock struck its last two notes after the library door had closed again.

" 'Curfew tolls the knell of parting day,' " Courtney Durbin said softly. "What's the last line?—'And leaves the world to darkness and to me.' "

She sat there silently for a few moments.

"Well," she said, "—so men live, and so men die. I wonder what they'll do to me. Hang me, I suppose."

I looked at her in blank dismay. The emphasis, what there was, was on the "hang" . . . as if she weren't questioning

74

the accuracy of Justice at all, merely inquiring about the modus. It was a little sickening.

"He was dead," she said. She stared straight in front of her into the fireplace, her voice an even colorless monotone. "—Strangled, I imagine. His face . . . looked like it. Right in his chair, there at his desk. No wonder the house has been so quiet. It's always quiet. That's one of the things I've hated about it. Never a sound. All the walls so insulated it was like living in padded cells. You could look out of the window and see children playing and dogs barking—you knew they were barking and the children laughing—but you couldn't hear it. Sometimes it almost drove me mad. It was like being dead."

"Stop it, Courtney," I said. "Don't. There's no use now."

"No, not now," she said. "You're right. The less I say the better off I'll be."

I had the same creeping chill up my spine I'd had the moment before. Then I had a gruesome and terrible idea, suddenly, and I looked sideways at her hands. But that was out. She couldn't possibly have used those hands for any such grisly effort.

"Where's Duleep Singh?" she asked abruptly, without moving.

"I don't know," I said. "We left him at the Blodgetts'. Why?"

"He told me once I was facing a black wall. He could see it in front of me. I asked him what was on the other side. He couldn't see anything there, he said. Nothing but the black wall. That's all I can see right now."

She stopped for a moment.

"Do you think people can see those things?"

"No," I said. "Don't be silly."

I wasn't as positive as I was trying to sound. I was beginning to be a little disturbed about Duleep Singh. People's lives may be open books, but there's no use for those who can read them to go around doing it aloud. Unless, of course, there was a reason behind it. I began to wonder. If Duleep Singh could see black walls, perhaps he'd seen the one in front of D. J. Durbin, and that was why he hadn't showed up.

In any case, there was no use of Courtney's allowing fear or hope to make her try to escape the reality she was faced with. That was what had happened to Corinne Blodgett. It was hard to imagine Courtney Durbin ever going fey and wearing a coarse linen robe and subsisting on dates and goat's milk, but it must have been hard for Corinne's contemporaries to imagine her doing it too, and she hadn't had anybody as attractive as Duleep around to lead her into it.

75

Though I still couldn't see him in his role of Swami. He must have reserved it for very special audiences. The nearest I'd ever come to being part of one was at the Abbotts' the night before. Even then, the idea of blood on the moon when it's full and sultry red on the evening horizon isn't particularly startling or bizarre. Especially if you've ever been to Charleston and heard the old blind minstrel on the Battery singing "When the moon goes down in blood and the saints come marching home" it isn't. On the other hand, Courtney had risen instantly to the bait, if bait there'd been, in his saying it. She may have thought he was speaking in some kind of parable for her especially. And of course, I thought, he may have been.

"I don't really believe it," she said. "But it's odd he should have said it out of a clear sky the way he did. It was the second time he was ever in this house. I didn't know I was making such a bad job of it. I knew the black wall was in front of me, but I didn't know anyone else could see it."

She turned her head and looked across the hall, her face contracted in a spasm of sudden despair.

"Oh, why don't they come out! What are they doing! I can't stand it much longer, Grace—I'll go mad if they don't come!"

The door opened then and Colonel Primrose did come out, Inspector Bigges and Horace Blodgett with him. Inspector Bigges was speaking, with the air of a man who was giving in but was not convinced.

"—You're the doctor, Colonel. If you say so it's all right. I'm not sticking my neck out any more than I have to, and I know Mr. Blodgett's reputation. But Mr. Blodgett knows as well as I do he didn't have any right——"

Horace's voice was dry, steady and patient.

"That document was taken from my office by someone, Inspector. When I heard about this meeting here this evening, I had reason to believe it would be here. When I opened this door and saw what had happened, my first idea —before anything else—was to find it. I did not do it in the interests of a private client, but in the interests of the people of this country, Inspector. I'm perfectly willing to turn it over to any competent authority who I know will keep its contents secret."

"All right, sir," Inspector Bigges said, still a little grimly. "You know how the newspapers are on my tail, Colonel. But let's get going. All set?"

The last was to a short man in a rumpled seersucker suit. I recognized him as Dr. Kettner, the medical examiner who used to come with Captain Lamb before Captain Lamb had the newspapers on his tail to the extent that he decided to go to war for a little peace and quiet. He beckoned to the

Inspector, and the two of them went back into the library, Colonel Primrose and Horace watching them. Inspector Bigges came out in a minute, and the three of them came across the hall, together with a middle-aged man with a dictation pad and pencil in his hand.

Colonel Primrose waited until they were in the drawing room, and closed the door. From the way he did it, glancing back at the library, I knew that very shortly now D. J. Durbin would be leaving his house on that last grim journey to the dust. There was a moment's silence.

"You met Inspector Bigges this afternoon, I think, Mrs. Durbin," Colonel Primrose said.

From the Inspector's expression I didn't know whether he hadn't connected the Mrs. Durbin at the Cranes' with this one, or just didn't recognize her for the same woman.

He nodded. "What is the matter with your hands, Mrs. Durbin?" he asked shortly.

I felt sorry for her. It was so hard to say baldly what had happened. She must have felt a natural reluctance, when the coroner's men were probably in the very act of taking away the body of the man whose name she had—along with the imposing luxury that surrounded her—to point through the black wall and say, "He did it."

"She was trying to save the kitten I told you about," Colonel Primrose said. "That stick in there came down on her hands."

She looked at him gratefully. Inspector Bigges made no comment.

"There doesn't seem to be any doubt, I'm afraid, Courtney," Colonel Primrose said, "that Mr. Durbin was murdered . . . strangled. You must have realized it . . ."

She moved her head in assent. She'd pulled herself together to an extent that would have amazed them if they'd seen her when Inspector Bigges and his men came, and if they didn't know her as well as I did.

"We don't want to distress you any——"

"I know, Colonel Primrose. I'm glad to help any way I can. Don't try to . . . to save my feelings."

Inspector Bigges looked relieved. He'd probably expected histrionics, if not hysteria . . . and in a sense, I rather thought, he was getting them without recognizing the difference between the dramatic types. Courtney was putting on a better show than he had any notion of, aware as she was—and as he was not—of the four discs on the green felt turntable of the victrola directly in front of his nose.

"When did you finish dinner, Courtney?" Colonel Primrose asked.

"We didn't have dinner," she answered calmly. "After the kitten episode Mr. Durbin was extremely upset. He called

77

Flowers and cancelled dinner, and told him to bring sandwiches and Scotch and soda to the library. He told me to go upstairs and soak my hands in hot water. I was afraid they were broken, but he didn't want a doctor called. One of the men—Mr. Skagerlund—tried to insist."

She shrugged her shoulders.

"Mr. Durbin wasn't in a state of mind anyone could . . . disregard. They went to the library and I went upstairs. The maid helped me undress, and taped my hands. That's all I can tell you. I didn't hear any disturbance down here, not until you people came. I was packing a bag then to leave. The reason—one reason—I was glad to see you was I thought Mr. Durbin would probably make it difficult if he knew I was leaving."

"What about your guests———"

"Mr. Skagerlund and Mr. Austin?"

She shook her head.

"I never met them till this evening. They were friends—or associates—of Mr. Durbin. I don't know anything about them. Mr. Skagerlund was very kind to me this evening . . . or tried to be. He didn't seem as afraid of Mr. Durbin as the other one."

Colonel Primrose was looking at her very intently.

"When did they leave, Courtney?"

Her voice was as calm and casual as his.

"I didn't know they had. I thought they were still there when Mr. Blodgett went in."

If I hadn't known she wasn't telling the truth just then I would never have suspected it. And I knew she wasn't because of the four black discs on the phonograph open over by the window . . . for she would never have been in the agony of despair she'd been in, suddenly remembering the recording machine, if the only people whose voices might be heard on it were two men she'd never seen until seven o'clock that evening. There are few things you can say with certainty in times like these, but that was definitely one of them. What she said sounded so true, however, that it made me wonder how much of anything else she'd said had been so.

"Then you saw him last———?"

"About twenty minutes to eight, when I went upstairs."

"And you didn't hear anyone come in or go, or any disturbance in the library?"

She shook her head. "That doesn't mean anything, however, as far as the library's concerned. It's insulated and practically soundproof. I didn't hear anyone at the door at all, before you came. Flowers may have."

"Is there a bell?"

She pointed to it at the side of the mantel. Colonel Primrose pressed it.

"When did it . . . happen?" she asked quietly. "Do you know?"

There was a moment's silence.

"That . . . is one of the questions," Inspector Bigges said.

Flowers must have been hovering very close to the back stairs, or come very fast. He was in the doorway, and he was not looking himself at all. His face had lost its high ebony gloss as if someone had dusted it with putty-colored flour. And a second dependable truth was clearly established, I thought, as he came in—or a second and a third truth. One was that he had not known when we came that D. J. Durbin was dead. The other was that he did now. That knowledge had shattered his dignified elegance like a bombshell on the fancy front of a jerry-built palace of fun. Flowers was reduced to original stem and bud. The bloom was gone, and with it, oddly enough, all the polysyllabic vocabulary.

14

"Tell Colonel Primrose anything you can, Flowers," Courtney said. "And don't be alarmed."

"I ain't alarmed, miss, I'm just plain scared," he said. "All them police downstairs . . ."

"They won't hurt you," Colonel Primrose said quietly. "When did you take the sandwiches to the library?"

"Eight o'clock on the dot, Colonel, sir. And that was the last time I saw Mr. Durbin, the very last time. He told me to get the hell out and downstairs and stay till he rung, and he ain't never rung. I didn't come out of the cellar till you kep' on ringin' the doorbell, and I thought he'd be out and raisin' cain, which is why I come up then."

"No one else came?"

"No, *sir.*"

"When did the two gentlemen leave?"

"I don't know *is* they left," Flowers said emphatically. "I didn't hear nobody come, or nobody go. And that's the truth, Colonel, sir."

"What about the other servants——"

"There ain't no other servants, sir. They left, and they're not coming back. The cook put the dinner in the icebox and went home. The maid and Mis' Durbin's maid left right afterwards. They say they don' use to work for crazy people."

Courtney shrugged her shoulders.

"You can't blame them."

She got up slowly and stood there for a moment.

"If you don't mind, I'd like to go to bed," she said. "I'm very tired. In the morning I'll talk to you again, but now

I'm tired.—Mr. Durbin's life was something I knew almost nothing about. He never discussed his business, or his family. . . . May I go now?"

I don't mean to sound as feline as I know I must, and it isn't feline, actually, as much as it's just a sound crimino-sociological observation, in view of the next few minutes. But Courtney Durbin all but had Colonel Primrose and Inspector Bigges making a rose-garlanded litter to bear her up the stairs. There was something so fragile and intangibly wistful in her appeal. It was so without artifice. She was tired, which was no doubt true, but the impression was she'd stay there till she dropped if they really wanted her to, which I'd have bet practically everything wasn't true. Only a brute could have said, "Hold everything, lady. You wait till we're through with you." She looked so ingenuous and so entirely in their hands, without laying on one thousandth of an inch more than the traffic would bear.

The men had got to their feet.

"Sure, you ought to try to get some rest," Inspector Bigges said hastily, because it was he she was looking at. He looked as if he felt like a dirty dog, keeping her there that long.

She took a step or two toward the door, and then, as if it had just occurred to her, she turned back, glancing at Colonel Primrose.

"It wouldn't disturb anyone if I turned on the victrola upstairs, would it?" she asked.

She went over to the open phonograph, picked up the records on the turntable as if she'd been playing them before all this, and started back to the door. There wasn't the slightest change in the delicate drooping line of her body or in the tempo of her movements. I sat there in a plain dither of suspense, feeling like a dirty dog myself, and with reason. It was a filthy trick I was playing on Colonel Primrose, who's a much better friend of mine than Courtney is. I had a definite idea, however, that he'd stop her and take the records away. I've got so used to his absolute omniscience. And when he moved a few steps in front of her to the door, I knew it was functioning. I was sorry in a way, because I knew the agony that was going on inside her.

She had about ten feet to go. It seemed a hundred to me, and I knew it seemed a hundred times that to her. I tried hard to breathe normally. And finally she was there. She held out her hand, then remembered and let it fall to her side.

"Good night, Colonel," she said. "Thank you for being here."

She turned to us.

"Good night, Grace. If you wouldn't mind staying all night, the blue room's ready, and I have anything you need Good night, Mr. Blodgett . . . Inspector."

I thought for a moment that Colonel Primrose was looking at the black discs under her arm, and that he was going to stop her. But he didn't; he just held the door open for her to go out. I could hear her steps on the stairs. The impulse to break and run like mad must have been intolerable, but she kept going more slowly, as if the physical effort of the long pull up was a little more than she finally had strength for. It was as perfect as it could possibly have been.

I didn't realize that I'd been holding my breath until I had to let it out again. It sounded to me like steam escaping from a pressure valve in an overheated laundry. But that was because the rest of them were so silent.

Colonel Primrose came back to us.

"She ought to have a doctor look at those hands," Inspector Bigges said practically. "It's a damned shame. I don't wonder she's getting out. I wouldn't blame her much if she'd . . ."

He came to a full stop, looking at Colonel Primrose with the most extraordinary expression on his face.

I've heard a lot of detectives say they didn't know what it was, but just something seemed to tell them. They never call it intuition, it's just something.

Surprise, doubt and deadly suspicion were dawning on Inspector Bigges's face like a tropical sunrise hung up over the eastern horizon. He shook his head as if coming out from under the influence of a spell, which I imagine is in fact just what he was doing, and got slowly to his feet.

"Say, Colonel . . ."

Colonel Primrose was looking at him gravely.

"I know," he said. He shot a disturbed and mistrusting glance at me. "I don't like it either. I think it's time we had a look around this place. We should have done it before, I expect."

He looked at me again, and raised his head, listening. From upstairs came the moving strains of Tschaikowsky's Sixth Symphony, barely audible, as if her door were closed.

He glanced across the hall, went to the library door and opened it. Then he turned back.

"I'd like you to have a look here, Mrs. Latham."

I thought at first he was being kind because he knew I was like the Spartan lad with the fox, my vitals being devoured by curiosity. But I made a mistake. That wasn't it, or anywhere near it.

I knew before I went in that D. J. Durbin would be gone, but I wasn't prepared for the rest of it. The room was as large as the drawing room, mahogany panelled, with a thick Persian rug on the floor, heavy dark green curtains pulled over the long windows at the front, and not a breath of air stirring anywhere, not even through the open windows onto

81

the terrace. I knew all that, and knew the two inside walls were lined with books—sets, mostly, quite new—and that his broad-topped mahogany desk was in the middle of the floor, facing the Grinling Gibbons reproduction fireplace and carved overmantel. What I didn't expect to see were the panels on either side of the fireplace open and revealing filing cabinets I didn't know were there, and the two leather chairs that had been drawn up between the fireplace and the desk and pushed back again, one of them so violently it had knocked over the Jacobean chair behind it.

By each chair was a small table, on it a plate, a linen napkin and a highball glass. The highball glasses were still full, the napkins untouched. Each plate had a sandwich on it, and only one sandwich had a bite out of it. The bread was curled up, the lettuce drooping unattractively around the edges. On the desk was a large silver plate with more sandwiches, and a decanter and syphon.

Also on the desk, in front of D. J. Durbin's chair, was a plate with another untouched sandwich, and a highball glass lying on its side on a large completely soggy dark green blotting pad. Mr. Durbin's stick was there too. It lay broken in half on the desk, the ink from the crystal stand there dried, bronze-edged, where it had slopped over onto it.

Even without D. J. Durbin sitting in that chair, strangled, they'd said, so that his tongue must have protruded horribly, and his eyes too, I still found myself stopping short in the door, the way Horace Blodgett and Colonel Primrose had done. It was a mute but living picture of three men who had started out with at least an appearance of amicability, and had ended with murderous violence. I saw at once why neither Inspector Bigges nor Colonel Primrose had been as on guard with Courtney as they might under other circumstances have been.

I think the three men standing just behind me all started, as I did, when the phone on the desk buzzed sharply, like something hidden and alive speaking out in a place of the dead.

Inspector Bigges pushed past me and picked it up before it had time to ring again.

"Hello," he said. "Speaking."

He nodded to Colonel Primrose as if it were a call they'd been expecting.

"You've checked everywhere?"

After that it was a series of monosyllables, mostly yeses, the frown on his face etching itself deeper with each one.

"The hell you say," he said at last. "Give it everything you've got."

He put the phone down and turned around. I had the unpleasant feeling that my presence was a definite repressive, because usually when there's that light in a man's eye there are words on his tongue to match it.

"Blown," he said. "Both of 'em. The boys got there in five minutes, and hung around both entrances for half an hour before they went inside. The lady says they left at a quarter to seven and haven't been back."

I knew of course he must mean the two men who'd been in this room, and when I looked at Colonel Primrose he nodded without saying anything.

"—They've checked the airport and they're working on the station."

Colonel Primrose looked at his watch. "It's not late. They may show up."

Inspector Bigges shook his head. "The lady said one of them called up the maid and asked her to bring their brief-cases down to the Garfield Hotel. That was around quarter past nine. The maid hasn't come back and she's not at her cousin's house. They haven't been able to get hold of the doorman who was on duty at the Garfield. It's my guess they've cleared out, Colonel."

His gaze moved past us to Horace Blodgett.

"If Mr. Blodgett would loosen up a little about who those men are . . ." he began deliberately.

I thought Colonel Primrose hesitated for a moment be-fore he spoke, but Horace said nothing.

"Cass Crane, I expect, is the man who can tell us more about them. In fact——"

Inspector Bigges nodded grimly as he interrupted.

"—In fact, Cass Crane can tell us more about lots of things. He can tell us a better story about what happened to that little driver. Cass Crane or somebody else. That story won't wash any longer, Colonel."

I caught my breath. It may not sound very bright, but for some reason I can't fully explain I hadn't until that very moment connected the murder of Achille, in the slight-est degree, with the violent death that had taken place in the room we were standing in, not two hours before. It may be that when Colonel Primrose said they were going to arrest D. J. Durbin for the little man's murder, that had finished that for me. I'd never known him to be wrong, and never known him to take a final action unless his case was proved.

"—Throws the whole stinking business right back where it began," Inspector Bigges said morosely.

What the implications were, and how staggering they were, I realized as they took form slowly out of the complete fog my mind seemed to be in. It wasn't so much that it was all back where it had begun as that where it had begun was the little white house in Beall Street.

"And I'd like to know who sent that kitten," Inspector

Bigges added. "That's a screwball trick, if we were looking for one."

Randy Fleming had called Mr. Sondauer a screwball . . . that flashed into my mind, bringing a momentary small ray of what looked like light. I glanced quickly at Colonel Primrose, but he shook his head, so I kept still. I couldn't understand him. I'd never seen him so silent, and so willing, apparently, to let somebody else take the full burden of an investigation.

Inspector Bigges stood there chewing one corner of his lower lip, intent on something going on in his own mind. He came back to the door, looked over toward the staircase for a moment and turned back to Colonel Primrose.

"There's one thing I've always found it didn't pay to overlook, Colonel," he said speculatively. "I don't know as it comes in here. But . . . she's a damned attractive woman."

He nodded toward the upper stairs. Then he turned and glanced at D. J. Durbin's desk.

"Because of what's happened here, she's free to marry somebody else . . . if she happens to *want* to marry somebody else. Free as air, Colonel . . . and with a wad of dough. And I mean a wad."

Colonel Primrose was looking intently at me, a curious ghost of a smile in his black eyes. I knew at once that he'd thought of that already, and that he knew I hadn't. And I knew that without saying it he was putting a choice of loyalties up to me. Molly Crane, or Courtney Durbin.

"Yes," he said quietly. "You're quite right. It doesn't pay to overlook it. She's a very attractive woman, and she'll probably be a very wealthy one. It's . . . apt to be a winning combination."

I thought of Molly playing checkers on the floor at the Abbotts', and Randy Fleming picking the hair from her paint brush out of the uneven blob of paint on the living room mantelpiece . . .

Inspector Bigges nodded.

"She's got everything it takes. It looks to me as if somebody sure did her a favor."

His eyes met Colonel Primrose's.

"This fellow Crane, now. I'd like to know what he was doing tonight . . ."

He stopped short as the front door opened and shut. A uniformed policeman came down the hall.

"A couple of guys out here want to know if they can come in, Inspector. They say they're friends of the Colonel's."

"Who are they?"

"One's named Crane and the other's some kind of a foreigner. Sounds like 'Sing,' or something."

"Sure, let 'em in," Inspector Bigges said genially. "Glad to see 'em."

His glance as he turned and looked at Colonel Primrose was what Flowers before his bloom was gone would have called full of signification.

15

Neither Cass Crane nor Duleep Singh made any attempt to conceal that he knew D. J. Durbin was dead. In fact it was openly the reason they'd come, or that Cass had. Duleep Singh didn't say why he was there and I can't recall anybody asking him.

"Mrs. Durbin just phoned," Cass said. He came down the hall. "Is she . . . all right?"

Of course heat makes anyone seem washed out. When it's hotter at ten minutes past eleven at night that it is at twelve noon most people look like dishrags. When Cass said he'd been in the Pentagon in the morning, and again part of the evening, that without the heat was enough explanation for why he looked the way he did. The Greeks had a story for it . . . though it's highly probable that compared with the War Department's job across the Potomac the Minoan labyrinth was a friendly boxwood maze set between the croquet green and the orangery in an old-fashioned garden. Perhaps too the fact that Duleep Singh was used to hot weather and hadn't been in the Pentagon, and looked cool and freshly laundered, made Cass Crane look more disheveled and fagged out than he really was. And he was naturally disturbed about Courtney, which Duleep Singh was not.

What I mean is, there were a lot of perfectly simple reasons for the impression Cass made if Inspector Bigges had bothered to find them. It's one of the troubles of preconceived ideas. Inspector Bigges a few moments before had reversed the French axiom into "cherchez l'homme," having the femme already, and was more than open to the conviction that he had searched, and found. Courtney's phoning Cass the minute she got upstairs and his slight hesitation in asking if she was all right, plus the fact that he looked as if he'd been drawn through an emotional as well as physical knothole, made it the most natural assumption in the world when anyone was hellbent on making an assumption.

I could understand it in Inspector Bigges. I was surprised to see Colonel Primrose apparently doing the same thing. He gave me a gentle push forward out of the library doorway and pulled the door shut behind him. It was the most effective gesture he could possibly have made to establish his solidarity with the Law, as opposed to what had seemed to me, anyway, his definite appearance of being on Cass's side of the invisible fence. He was perfectly affable, however. It was he who said Courtney was all right, that she was holding up very well, that she'd presumably gone to bed. He spoke to Duleep Singh and introduced him to the Inspector.

He nodded toward the drawing room. "If you gentlemen will come in here, there are a few questions we'd like to ask you. Perhaps you and Mr. Blodgett and ourselves can get together on some of this."

As they started across, Cass glanced up the stair well. Whether his anxiety came from solicitude or misgiving I didn't know. I'm sure at that angle he couldn't see the small segment of ivory lace flaring through the mahogany standards that I could see . . . and that I was instantly aware Colonel Primrose had seen. As my eye caught his I realized that he must have been watching Courtney all the time. There was a mirror on the wall at the turn of the stairs, and she'd been standing where she could see us down by the library door, forgetting, if she'd known it, something Colonel Primrose pointed out to me a long time ago; if you can see anyone's eyes in a mirror, they can also see you in it. I suppose because the light behind her was off she didn't realize there was enough thrown up from the lower hall to show her shadowy watching figure visible in the glass.

It all flashed through my mind so quickly, and with it a half-formed visual image emerging out of my own unconscious, that I took a step back to verify it. Or I started to, and found myself politely and unobtrusively blocked. Colonel Primrose smiled a little, and I didn't go back and look again to find out I was *quite* right. And maybe it was just because she wanted to see Cass. If I could complain because Inspector Bigges and Colonel Primrose weren't giving him the benefit of the doubt, I shouldn't myself refuse to give it to Courtney. But it was so unwise of her. It made all the rest of the part she'd played so exquisitely, down in this room, suddenly and patently false. It would have been so much better if she'd just come downstairs.

If Horace Blodgett had so much as nodded to Duleep Singh, I hadn't noticed it. It was Cass he was looking at.

"—Is it true that Lons Sondauer is in town?"

"I guess it is. I didn't know it—exactly—until tonight."

It sounds as if I'm trying to make a fool out of Inspector Bigges, saying that his eyes lighted up instantly. And I'm not, because he was really a superior officer and intent on his job. And after all, having the entire available detective force out hunting for Mr. Lons Sondauer it's natural he'd be interested.

"How did you find it out, Crane?"

"A friend of mine, Lieutenant Fleming, told me," Cass said. "He'd met him in Egypt, and ran into him here the other day."

Inspector Bigges nodded. "All right. I want to know who this guy Sondauer is."

Cass Crane looked at him deliberately across the point of flame he was holding up to his cigarette. He snapped his lighter shut and took the cigarette out of his mouth.

"It just goes to show you don't know the best people, Inspector," he said ironically, shaking his head. "Or . . . maybe not. *I'd* never heard of him till I got this job. But take the old boy who got bumped off in the Bahamas. The papers said he was worth two hundred million and I'd never heard of him either. They tell me money isn't everything, after all. Well, Sondauer is that sort of a guy, Inspector. He's what the papers call a man of mystery. And I guess that's about all I can tell you."

"You mean that's all you know about him?"

"No, Inspector."

He looked at Bigges thoughtfully for a moment.

"I know a lot about him. I've been on his trail for four months. But . . . it's just not for publication, Inspector."

It sounded like a definite period to me.

Colonel Primrose spoke very suavely. "I'm afraid you'll have to open up a little, Cass. Durbin was murdered tonight. Sondauer was in the house."

Cass moved abruptly. "Sondauer here? Tonight?"

He sounded surprised, and skeptical.

"The man Randy says is Sondauer was here."

"But I thought——"

Cass stopped short. Whether he was thinking fast or just hard, I wouldn't know. He turned to Inspector Bigges.

"This is very much off the record, then. Okay?"

He hesitated an instant.

"Mr. Sondauer," he said slowly, "is one of the birds you never hear about. You've never even heard his name. But if you threw out everything you use that he's got a finger in, from getting rid of a headache to driving your car to Headquarters, you'd be back in a covered wagon and no axle grease. He's one of the biggest spiders in the web they're beefing about, Inspector, when they talk about international cartels."

"What's he doing here?" Inspector Bigges asked bluntly.

A flicker moved in Cass's gray eyes for an instant. Then he grinned broadly.

"Don't be naive, Inspector. Though if you mean what's he

doing in Washington today, I couldn't tell you. He's not here officially until next Monday. He's here then to see if he can shake loose a couple of million dollars' worth of equipment, and shipping space for it, for a project he's got in . . . a place called 'X.' I might as well tell you he got here on the same plane I did. He just didn't happen at that time to know I was the guy he wanted to see. When he found it out, did he want to kick himself around."

He grinned with cheerful amusement.

Inspector Bigges hesitated.

"Would he have business with Durbin?"

Cass's short laugh was not so amused.

"Brother, he would. If he could get Durbin to loose his stranglehold, he'd be all set—if he could get me to change my report. That's all Sondauer needed. And that's one angle, Inspector. The other is maybe he found out he'd already been double-crossed and all D. J. Durbin needed was to keep my report from going in at all. In either case, plenty of business with Durbin. And not much to lose. When the Japs wiped out Sondauer's assets in Burma, they left Durbin holding the balance of power . . . in a game of dog eat dog, with Mr. Sondauer's elongated bicuspids snapped off at the middle. In fact, Inspector, you're sitting right now in the former drawing room of the real king pin man of mystery in this outfit."

Inspector Bigges waited with a kind of dogged patience.

"D. J. Durbin's the real man nobody knows," Cass said. His irony was a little grimmer. "He's the nigger in the stockpile. The minute you get your finger on him, he's gone or he wasn't there. You know he's the guy that hamstrings everything you try to do so you can only do half of it, and the simple reason is he's sitting tight waiting to move in on the post-war setup. He gives out just enough to keep from being blacklisted and running the risk of confiscation when we win. Nobody knows what he's in, or where. If it hadn't been for a little matter of an airport, we'd never have got him. And that was a fluke. Nobody even thought he was in the picture."

He aimed his cigarette butt carefully at a point in the middle of the fireplace and let it go.

"It was an airport eight hundred and fifty miles from Bogotá. He had it all fixed—or he thought he did—for us to build it to get out the stuff we need now. Then we'd abandon it when the war was over and he'd have it. A Berchtesgaden in the middle of a modern El Dorado. It looked fine on paper, and as long as nobody suspected Durbin was in it, nobody said boo. A lot of other interests had their eye on next Armistice Day too, ready to grab. Nobody knew Durbin had it all set and tied up, so when we got in there

88

we'd find we couldn't get enough stuff out to pay for the gas it took to get a plane in. It was neat as hell. He had the whole thing right in the palm of his hand. If it hadn't been me they sent down to look it over, nobody would have connected him with it in a thousand years—or until the day peace was signed rather."

He grinned at us again.

"—It wasn't because I was smart. It just happened I had a background not many other people would have. He didn't use the name Durbin down there, but . . ."

He stopped suddenly, as if thinking better of that.

"Anyway, I washed him up," he said. "He was willing to pay out to fix me up, too. And friend Sondauer, working on his own little scheme, didn't know his friend Durbin was cutting the ground out from under him. He also doesn't know that when he turns up in Washington next Monday the black arm band out of respect for his old brother-in-arms isn't going to get him to first base."

I could see Inspector Bigges trying to boil all this down to a soft ball forming in water that he could get hold of for his own purposes.

"He'd have plenty of reason for wanting Durbin out of the way?"

Cass's smile was pleasant, and detached.

"That, Inspector," he said, "is what is called, tritely, a masterpiece of understatement. I couldn't tell you how many times he's tried it already . . . and vice versa. In the places those boys roam a little thing like getting a murder done costs about as much as a good five-cent cigar, and it's a lot easier to get. Durbin's accident is supposed to have been one of Sondauer's playful little jobs. He's a great wag, Inspector. Always full of practical jokes, like putting breakfast food in your bed on the plane. They say the trouble is you can't always tell whether it's just good clean fun."

He paused, and went on looking at Inspector Bigges deliberately.

"People who know him tell me there are those who'd die of thirst before they'd take a drink he's had a chance at. That's the gossip on the foreign Rialto. Sometimes you get the impression he's just a screwball, other times that a nice cobra would be more fun to have around. I don't know, myself. I can tell you one thing—he's shrewd as hell. I talked to him a lot on the plane. All I got was he was just out for the ride, and a devil with women on six continents. I mentioned Durbin once, just for fun, but he'd never heard of him."

He got to his feet.

"That's as explicit as I'm allowed to be about him, Inspector. He must have found out after he left the plane who I

89

was. One thing more: I didn't know Durbin knew he was due here. I sent up a trial balloon on that too, and Durbin wanted to know if he'd said whether he expected to come to Washington. And Julie Ross told my wife the Durbins had arranged, way last week, for him and some guy with him to stay at her house. These people don't let anybody else's right hand know what their left one's doing.—Well, I came over to see if there was anything I could do for Mrs. Durbin."

"Just a minute," Inspector Bigges said. "When did you see Durbin last? This bribe he offered you. . . . When——"

"It wasn't anything as crude as a bribe, Inspector," Cass said. "It was a golden opportunity, for a young man of parts . . . beginning as of January 1st, this year. That was last night. Mrs. Durbin met me at the plane. We went to the Abbotts' to find my wife, and dropped in here then to phone around and see if we could locate her. I didn't expect to see Durbin, because it's . . . important to my job that I didn't seem to be tied up with him. I couldn't refuse to come in, on the other hand, since they've been friendly. I've been here a lot without his smelling a rat—I think. He knew I'd been down in his bailiwick, all right. I knew he would. But he didn't know for sure whether I knew it was his. Or I don't think he did. He did a first-rate job of trying to find out, and he was a hell of a lot smarter than I am, so maybe I gave it away without knowing it."

He put his cigarette on the silver ashtray this time, and looked up at Colonel Primrose.

"I didn't know, as I told you, whether Achille's body in my house meant Durbin had figured out I knew he was it, or whether he just wanted to make sure I didn't spill the general dope on the business. But when he gets bumped off himself . . ."

He shrugged his shoulders.

"Sondauer was at my house earlier. Maybe it wasn't Durbin. I guess Sondauer would be just as interested in what I'd brought back with me as Durbin would."

"—Meaning?" Inspector Bigges demanded.

"Somebody had taken a look through my bags in the back of the Durbin's car, while I was inside the house. I found that out when I got home and started to unpack."

"Anything missing?"

"No."

He turned back to Colonel Primrose. "If that's all I'll be getting back. Will you tell Mrs. Durbin, if you see her before you go, that I'll be around in the morning?"

He started to the door and stopped.

"I wonder if I could speak to you a minute, Colonel?"

The two of them went out into the hall, Colonel Primrose closing the door.

16

Inspector Bigges chewed the corner of his lower lip, and the rest of us just sat there. I don't know how long it was before Colonel Primrose put his head in the doorway.

"Bigges—look here, will you?" he said.

I had a strange feeling in the pit of my stomach. It was the way he'd spoken, and the total disappearance of the suave urbanity that he usually had even when the going was tough. I glanced at Duleep Singh. Not for any reason that I was aware of, except that I wanted to look somewhere. He was looking at me, which may have been why I felt my eyes drawn to his. There was a sombre almost hypnotic quality about him that held me a moment, so that I had the feeling that his eyes had been fixed on me for some time, quietly dissecting me when I didn't know it.

He smiled at me. I don't know whether he was seeing a black wall in front of me, but he must have seen I was disturbed. He didn't, however, have to be a swami to see that, I'm afraid, because even Horace Blodgett, the newt-souled, saw it.

"What's the matter, Grace?" he asked. "You haven't been . . . thwarting justice, have you?"

I didn't have a chance to answer, because at that instant Colonel Primrose put his head in the door again and said, "Mrs. Latham."

If Sergeant Phineas T. Buck could have heard him, all his fears that his colonel had been or ever could be an Odysseus to my Circe would have vanished forever. He'd never spoken to me so sharply in all our association. I can't think of anybody else who has either. There was something in my throat that made it hard for me to swallow.

"Come here, please," he said curtly.

I went out into the hall.

Inspector Bigges was angry too. And Cass Crane stood in the middle of the hall looking as flabbergasted as somebody who'd unwittingly pulled a chair out from under the archbishop. That he hadn't intended what he'd done to have the effect it had was perfectly evident, on the face of both it and him. I had an indescribable sinking feeling that of course it was the business of the records. And I was right. I knew it the instant I saw the door into the room beyond the stairs open and the light go on.

"Go upstairs, please, Mrs. Latham," Colonel Primrose said quietly, "and tell Courtney I want to see her."

There was no question about not doing it. I simply went.

Moreover, he and Inspector Bigges were about two steps behind me. Cass Crane, when I looked down, was still standing there, with a sort of what-the-hell-have-I-done-now expression on his face, not knowing whether to come or go.

I knocked at Courtney's door and opened it. Colonel Primrose and the Inspector stood to one side, in the interests of decency, I supposed. They needn't have bothered. Courtney was sitting at her desk, still in her lace robe.

"Come in," she said calmly. "Have they——"

I moved the muscles of my face around in what must have been an extraordinary grimace, and said, "Colonel Primrose is here. He wants to see you."

"Bring him in, by all means." She turned around in her chair. "What is it, Colonel?"

Perturbed as I was, it still struck me as a little funny seeing Colonel Primrose and Inspector Bigges bringing the strong arm and brazen hooves of constituted authority into the pastel sanctity of a lady's private sitting room. It looked like the pale inside of a seashell anyway, and they looked definitely as if they belonged somewhere else.

"Those records, Courtney," Colonel Primrose said. "I want them, immediately."

"——Oh, Colonel, I'm so sorry!"

She got to her feet.

"The most dreadful thing happened. I dropped them. They're broken simply to bits. They're here, in the basket."

She picked up the tole lily-shaped basket beside the desk and handed it to him.

When she said they were broken to bits she was speaking literally indeed. If she'd put them in a mortar and used a pestle on them they couldn't, in fact, have been broken into smaller bits.

Colonel Primrose held the ridiculous waste basket in his hands for a moment, looking down on the black ground-up mess in the bottom of it. His voice was controlled and quiet when he spoke, but his black eyes snapped with a look that would have shrivelled an armadillo's hide.

"You're going to regret this bitterly, Courtney," he said.

His steady tones stung like a cat-o'-nine-tails. I moved away a little, myself.

"It was the stupidest thing you could have done. It was criminally stupid. The only possible assumption anyone can make is that you know who murdered your husband, and you know his voice was recorded there. If you had set out deliberately to hang anyone, you couldn't have done a better job of it. Now go to bed . . . and if you know how to pray, pray God that someone can undo the harm you've done."

Courtney stood steadying herself against the desk, her face gray-green. At the door he turned.

"There'll be a guard downstairs tonight. You're to stay in this room until you're allowed to leave it. I'd like you to do a little quick serious thinking. There's such a thing as an accessory after the fact, and there are a lot of them serving terms in the women's penitentiaries.—Come along, Mrs. Latham. I'm going to take you home."

I guess it wasn't a black wall Duleep Singh had been seeing in front of me. It was just a long, long flight of stairs. I thought I'd never get to the bottom of it, with Colonel Primrose and Inspector Bigges clumping down behind me, and if I'd been walking up with a gallows' rope dangling at the top I couldn't have been unhappier. And I guess too that I was being allowed to do a little quiet thinking myself, because after Cass and Duleep Singh and Horace left the house together, he and the Inspector went back into the library and closed the door. If I hadn't been in the luxurious dog house of a drawing room he'd probably have let me be in there with them. But I'd been reduced to the ranks, in as summary a court-martial as anybody ever got.

I don't know how long I sat there, pretty shattered, trying to bind up my wounded vanity. It seemed a long time, but maybe it wasn't. It was very gradually, anyway, that I became aware there was somebody else somewhere fairly close to me. I could feel another presence as definitely as if I could see it. I sat there motionless, not daring to look round, chill creeping things moving along my spine. The place was so damned quiet. I couldn't hear a sound except my own heart, and all I could feel was a sharp terror at being alone and yet knowing that something else . . . I could hear it then, behind me toward the dining room, and I got to my feet and turned around, getting my hand to my mouth just in time to stifle what I know would have been a blood-curdling scream.

There was someone in the door. That wasn't just a product of overwrought nerves. But it was Molly Crane . . . and she looked a lot scareder than I was. Her eyes were like dark amber saucers and her face was so white and strained that it's a wonder I recognized her as quickly as I did. I looked frantically across the hall. The library door was still closed.

"What on earth are you doing here?" I whispered. "How did you get in?"

I went as close to her as I could and still keep an eye on the door. She crept in softly, keeping out of the line of it.

"—I've been here for *hours*," she whispered desperately. "I came the back way, and I can't get out. There's a policeman out there. What'll I do? I've got to get out—I've simply *got* to, before anybody finds me. Oh, Grace, think of something, quick!"

I suppose I must have just stood there staring at her.

"Grace, please! I've got to get out!"

Trying to think of something quick when the place was surrounded by policemen, and when I expected the library door to open any instant and Colonel Primrose walk out and see us, wasn't as easy as it may sound. The only people who could hope to get out would be the colored servants. It seems to me now I wasted hours trying to think of how she could black her face and pretend she was a maid. There was still her yellow hair and nothing plausible to tie around it, and anyway it was too fantastic.

I looked down at my dinner dress. If I could get her into that, I thought. But I'm taller than she is and even if I'd had very much under it, which I hadn't, Colonel Primrose would probably have noticed it. Then it occurred to me suddenly. The only possible thing to do was the obvious thing, and it had worked once that evening. It might again.

"Look, Molly," I said. "This is a chance, but you've got to take it. Go right to the front door and open it and walk out. Be quick, and as casual as you can. They can't hear from the library. They don't know outside who's here. And listen —*don't close the door clear shut*. Remember. And go quick!"

I didn't blame her for feeling her feet were glued to the floor, though I didn't know how really desperate her need for getting out was, except as I could see it in the pulse beating madly in her throat.

"If they stop you say you're the nurse. Anything. But go quick, darling."

She nodded, and the next minute she was going down the hall. I saw her body straighten as if she were bracing herself, and I didn't look at her again. My eyes were on the library door and my heart was in my mouth. I waited . . . a long time, it seemed to me, trying in my mind to see her reach the gate and then the sidewalk and turn and go down Massachusetts Avenue—almost to 22nd Street, I hoped she'd be, before I crossed the room and went out into the hall.

The door was almost closed, but not quite. I listened a moment. There was no sound except the policeman at the gate whistling. I pushed the door to.

Almost instantly the library door opened and Colonel Primrose looked out. His expression changed from inquiry to suspicion when he saw it was I.

"I thought I'd like a little air," I said.

He didn't smile.

"You go and sit down, Mrs. Latham," he said. "I'll take you home in about five minutes."

"I'd rather go now," I said.

He didn't say anything, but stood watching me until I went back to the drawing room. Then he left the library door ajar. I gathered that however tightly Mr. Durbin had insulated himself against noise, he still knew when anyone entered or left his house—from the front anyway. How Molly had got in, why she'd come, where she'd been all the time, how long she actually meant by "hours," . . . a dozen questions raced around in my mind as I sat down again to wait. There was only one thing I could be so completely sure of I didn't have to question it at all . . . and that was that even presuming she could possibly have strangled D. J. Durbin, she was the one person in the world who wouldn't want to. I wondered whether she'd been there long enough to hear Inspector Bigges say Courtney was as free as air, with a wad of dough . . . or hear Cass say he'd come to see if Mrs. Durbin was . . . all right.

It couldn't have been five minutes, actually, that I sat there going over it in my mind. Colonel Primrose and the Inspector came out, Bigges finishing something he'd started to say on the other side of the door.

"—case against Sondauer. I wonder if he had anything else in mind, Colonel. They say in the Army the best *de*fensive is a mighty powerful *of*fensive."

"We'll have to see," Colonel Primrose said. "Meanwhile, I'm going home. I'll see you in the morning."

He came to the drawing room door. "If you're ready, Mrs. Latham," he said without warmth.

17

It's invariably the obvious things you never gave a thought to that rise up and smite you. It's like taking elaborate precautions against cracking up in a helicopter and breaking your neck because you forgot there was ice on the front steps.

We were half-way down Courtney's front steps when Colonel Primrose said, "I wonder where Buck is?"

If I didn't trip and break my neck it was only because I was so dumfounded I couldn't.

"Buck?" I said.

He looked at me as if he thought the heat was responsible. "Certainly."

I hadn't thought of Sergeant Buck. When I sent Molly out the front way he never so much as crossed my mind. I suppose because he hadn't been visible at the Blodgetts' or standing by there inside Courtney's house, the wish was probably father to the thought that he'd somehow been permanently congealed and immobilized. If I'd stopped to think in rational terms I'd have known that an oyster doesn't go far without his shell or a shell without his oyster. Though the figure isn't apt except in the sense of common indispensability

. . . even if Colonel Primrose, very unlike himself, had kept a pretty oyster-like silence through the whole evening, except for his lashing of Courtney and its implied extension to me.

I was worried about Molly. Sergeant Buck would have recognized her, of course. Knowing Cass had come and left without her he'd naturally wonder what went on, and take matters in his own hands to find out. He'd also tell Colonel Primrose. Then there'd be more trouble.

"Well, we might as well walk," Colonel Primrose said, after looking around again. "If you're up to it."

"I could even run," I said.

As a matter of fact, I'd have liked to. There was a full-page advertisement in the papers that morning that had "Beware the Fury of a Patient Man" plastered across the top of it. It was in my mind then. To have to walk clear to Georgetown with him was not something I looked forward to.

We went about a block in complete silence. Then he took hold of my arm.

"Look, my dear," he said. "I'm sorry I was angry with you. But you know you're the most irritating woman I've ever known."

"I'm sorry," I said.

We both sounded contrite, although I was aware that under the newest circumstances my contrition reeked a little of the whited sepulchre.

"In fact, sometimes you're maddening. Let me tell you just one thing you helped do tonight. Cass Crane made the statement that Durbin tried to buy him off. It happens—for various reasons that are damned important—that that lies at the very heart of this affair. And Courtney Durbin destroyed the only actual positive evidence that that offer was made *and rejected*."

"I . . . don't know what you're talking about, really," I said.

"If you'll be quiet I'll tell you. Please, Mrs. Latham . . ."

He lapsed into a patient silence for a moment.

"Try to use your head just once, will you?" he said then, rather more like himself. "You know, if I wasn't very much in love with you, I'd think sometimes you have the I. Q. of a . . ."

He stopped again, fortunately. I don't know how low I could have stood for its being put, just then.

"Cass says he stopped by the Durbins' last night to call Molly. But we know Courtney met him at the airport. We know he'd let her and not his wife know he was coming in. He says himself that he was the one man who could put an okay or a rejection on this scheme of Durbin's. The thing they're dealing with happens to be of immense importance, Mrs. Latham. Well, the assumption could easily be—and you know Washington at the moment—that Cass Crane went straight to Durbin's to sell his goods. He gets fifty-six hundred a year. Durbin . . ."

He shrugged his shoulders.

"But don't be absurd, Colonel," I protested hotly. "You know very——"

"I asked you to be quiet, Mrs. Latham. Let's say this is Inspector Bigges' point of view—and he's not a fool by any means. Cass had the chance, last night, of taking charge of some of Durbin's interests and being an enormously wealthy man in a few years. Do you think he'd boggle at a small matter of simply keeping his mouth shut, because he's a gentleman and a friend of yours?"

"But . . . you said it was Durbin who was trying to kill Cass . . ."

He was silent for a moment.

"All right. Suppose, meanwhile, Cass had seen Courtney again, and saw she was more than willing to marry him if she could get free. It doesn't take much to see that. This is Bigges again.—It wasn't Durbin trying to poison Cass. It was Cass trying to poison Durbin. Durbin was at Cass's house last night, for one thing."

"How do you know he was there?" I demanded. "Nobody has——"

"By using my eyes. Next time you go to the Cranes' look at the floor, from where I looked sitting by the window. It takes a long time for shellac to dry in weather like this. You can see the marks of Durbin's stick straight down the middle of the room."

"Oh," I said.

"Furthermore, I saw Durbin at five o'clock this afternoon. He didn't say in so many words that he thought Cass was trying to give him a poisoned highball. He intimated he thought it was strange he'd call up a friend of his wife's to help him hide a body he wasn't responsible for. And he said, 'Of course you're aware of Crane's very personal interest in my wife.' "

We'd come to the Q Street bridge, with the grotesque buffaloes charging down at us from their pedestals. In the absence of traffic we could hear the burbling of Rock Creek coming up from below. It's been years since I was conscious of hearing it, very pleasant and uncity like. But Colonel Primrose wasn't interested in pastoral effects.

"Durbin's death," he went on deliberately, "—his murder —is all that's saved Cass Crane from complete ruin, as a matter of fact. The affair is that serious. Whether Cass is guilty or innocent, or Durbin guilty or innocent, Cass was going to get it. In another week he'd have been so smeared he couldn't have got along in this town. Whether he wrecked Durbin's plans, or Durbin was jealous about Courtney, or the unsavory shoe was on Cass's foot to begin with is no matter. Durbin had nothing to lose in terms that are understandable to us. His reputation was already what it was. He didn't need money. The whole power game was just a game. But it was one he was willing to stake other people's lives on. He was a ruthless man, in a sense that it's hard for a civilized human being to conceive."

"I'm afraid I don't really see quite what you're saying, Colonel," I said. "Maybe it's my I. Q., but——"

"I know," he said. "I'm not really saying anything. I'm just talking, my dear. Trying to clear it up in my own mind."

He hesitated, looking at me rather oddly.

"It happens I'm not primarily interested in murder, this time. Neither in Achille's nor in Durbin's. They're entirely incidental. I'm sorry for Achille, but so far as I'm concerned Mr. D. J. Durbin can rot in hell."

I looked at him blankly. It wasn't his language, though I'd never heard him say he didn't like someone quite so forcefully. But I certainly never expected to hear him say murder was incidental.

He took my arm again. "Do you think you could keep something to yourself?"

"No," I said. "It's a delusion I've abandoned, and I'm the only one who ever had it."   .

He chuckled.

"You can try, just once. If you can't bring yourself to help me you can at least stop trying to hinder me."

"All right," I said. "—Beginning as of now."

He looked sideways at me, a little doubtfully. But the advantage of being known to have a low I. Q. is that people don't think you really know what it is you're saying.

"The sole thing I'm concerned with is Cass Crane. And the answer was right there in those records . . . that you and Courtney were so helpful about."

"I wish," I said, "that you'd come right out and say what you mean. In words I can understand. I'm so tired of——"

"There have been a lot of rumors," he said quietly, "beginning about a month ago. They're either malicious, or true. They tend to discredit Crane completely. Nobody paid much attention to them until a story appeared in one of the gossip columns. It was to the effect that you could expect to see some of the bright young men who've investigated raw material sources coming out as post-war robber baronets, if they bothered to wait that long. It went on to say that if an ambitious young man was sent out to see whether the government should put a large sum of money at the disposal of a private group, or a foreign government, for the development

98

of needed strategic materials, it could be a great temptation —as well as a very easy matter—for him to look out for his own interests. There were strong hints tying the thing down to one man particularly."

He stopped for an instant, and went on.

"That's when I was called in, Mrs. Latham. I've been through Cass Crane's life since he got out of three-cornered pants . . . and through all his family ramifications."

"And so . . . ?" I asked.

"And so what?"

He shook his head.

"He got me out in the hall to ask if he could take over Durbin's records, before anyone else got to them. I thought he meant files, before he explained about Durbin's machine that recorded everything spoken in the library. Well, it could mean his conscience was clear and he was just on the job. It could also mean he was pretty anxious to get hold of them for his own purposes."

Courtney Durbin's terror when she suddenly thought of the machine came back to me. The new meaning it could have wasn't consoling.

"You assume," he said evenly, "that because a man's able, and a nice fellow, comes from your social group and is married to a friend of yours, that he's honest. I don't. And Bigges, who's trying to find out who killed those two people, doesn't either."

We'd turned down 29th Street and were passing his yellow brick house to cross over to my red brick one.

"It's Molly, as a matter of fact, I feel sorry for, right now," he said.

"Do you think Cass is in love with Courtney?" I asked abruptly.

He didn't answer right away—not until we'd stopped at my front door.

"Courtney's a fascinating woman," he said quietly. "She's a very rich one, and she's very smart. Molly's different. It's like expecting a cocker spaniel to beat a greyhound in a race for the butcher's cart. I . . . like the spaniel, myself. But Molly will be a fool, because she's young and in love and insecure. I don't know."

He added slowly, "I'm glad she's got Randy to fall back on. He's good goods, and so is she. Well, good night, my dear. I'm sorry—again."

He bent forward a little. I thought he was going to kiss me, and I still think he was. The lights of a car standing in front of the next house went on abruptly, the door opened, and a large man got out. There was no mistaking those massive shoulders outlined against the night. Sergeant Buck did not, however, turn his head and spit, and I thought it was rather sweet of him. He just came around the front of the car and opened the other door for Colonel Primrose.

"Figured I'd catch you here, sir."

He always talks out of one corner of his armor-plated mouth anyway, so it sounded more sinister and accusing than he meant it to . . . I hope.

Colonel Primrose smiled at me. "Good night, Mrs. Latham," he said.

Some day maybe Sergeant Buck will decide he should beware the fury of a patient man, to say nothing of the fury of an impatient woman. I add that to keep kind friends from adding it for me.

18

As a matter of fact, I was too concerned with other people's affairs just then to have more than a passing interest in my own.

If I'd been able to tell what Colonel Primrose really thought, what he meant by saying he was glad Molly had Randy to fall back on—and how far back she was going to have to fall—my mind wouldn't have been the rats' maze it was even after I got to sleep. I had one of those ghastly dreams that pick up all the undigested trifles of the day and make them into nightmare reality. I dreamed I was on a huge green felt turntable going round and around. Courtney and Cass, Inspector Bigges and Randy were on it with me, and Duleep Singh's eyes—just his eyes—were off to one side watching us. Corinne Blodgett kept coming in and out with her ration book in the form of yellow squash, hunting for Horace and Molly, getting everything confused just as it seemed to be on the point of becoming completely clear. I was glad when morning came.

At least I was till I looked at the paper. The front page screamed with the murder of D. J. Durbin, man of mystery and romance, and with his young and beautiful socialite wife, stricken by this terrible blow from the hand of the assassin. Where they'd unearthed the pictures of Courtney—child, debutante and bride—and of the house before, after and during D. J. Durbin's alterations of it, I'll never know. So far, and I was thankful for it, Cass's name didn't appear, or Molly's. The police were hunting the two men who were known to have been guests at dinner. There was a picture of Horace Blodgett, taken I'm sure from his college yearbook. He had found the body, and he was stricken too, it seemed. In fact everybody was at least stricken dumb, according to the reporters trying to explain why nobody would talk. One of them who'd called the Blodgett house said she'd talked to Mrs. Horace Blodgett, who'd said that of course her husband had never been a criminal lawyer so there must be some mistake. There was a picture of Inspector Bigges, a complete rehash of the reorganization of the detective bureau, and an account of how Inspector Bigges had got some Embassy's parrot out of a tree in Sheridan Square on New Year's Night.

Reading it over carefully a second time, I saw it boiled down to a simple statement that Horace Blodgett had found the dead body of D. J. Durbin, who was the husband of Courtney Durbin, that a Mr. Skagerlund and a Mr. Austin had been there to dinner, and that Inspector Bigges was in charge of the case. The rest of it was highly embroidered background to give the sweltering capital a little diversion from the war and the thermometer.

The only really interesting thing that I could see was a small box at the bottom of the front page. "Will the messenger boy who delivered the black kitten to a house on Massachusetts Avenue at seven o'clock last night please communicate with the police, for information only." It was the first real knowledge I had that either Colonel Primrose or Inspector Bigges, each working, apparently, on his own job, thought the kitten was genuinely relevant. And I might just as well say here that all they learned was that the kitten came from a pet shop on G. Street. It had been with four other various-colored animals in the box in the window with a "$2 Each" over it. On Wednesday morning when the proprietor opened the shop there was an envelope under the door. It had a five-dollar bill in it, and a note typed on a sheet of hotel stationery. The note asked him to send the black kitten in a shoe box to Mr. D. J. Durbin the next evening around seven o'clock, by hand, as a surprise, and to see that the messenger delivered it to Mr. Durbin himself. The extra three dollars was for the boy who took it. The proprietor had made a note of the address, thrown the original note in the waste paper basket and put the five dollars in the cash register. It was good business, because his first idea had been to drown the kittens, whose parents had obviously met in the alley behind the shop when the mother should have been catching mice inside.

And that was as far as that part of the investigation of the black kitten episode ever got. The alley itself couldn't have had a deader end. It took a whole day of a detective's time, and Colonel Primrose, as I learned, was the only person who thought it worth the trouble. And he, or so he'd said, was only incidentally interested in murder.

It was just on the stroke of eight when the phone by my bed rang. It was Molly.

"Grace," she said. Her voice sounded colorless and a little dead . . . very different from the frantic urgency that I'd heard in it last night.

"If you're not very busy this morning, would you come around? I'm going to be here. Cass has gone over to Courtney's."

I don't know why it struck me as being as incredible as it did. He'd said he was going to. But it seemed to me he ought to have more sense . . . or something. With what had happened, and particularly with all the gossip apparently going around, there'd be reporters and photographers sitting in the trees and under every stone you could turn over. My silence must have been obvious.

"It's all right, Grace," she said quickly. "You know they're very old friends. She . . . she really needs a man around to see to things. She hasn't any brothers."

"Well . . . of course, darling," I said hastily. "I think it's wonderful, and I'll be along after a while. Goodbye."

She was in the front room when I got there a little after half-past nine. She was sitting in the chair Courtney had sat in the day before. A small tray with half a grapefruit, a couple of pieces of toast and a cup of coffee was on a table by her. The cream had made a scum across the top of the coffee and the toast and grapefruit were untouched. She was slumped down on the middle of her spine, staring in front of her.

"Buck up, sweetie," I said.

I found myself looking quickly at the floor, and wondering how I'd been so blind. Even in the morning light the round marks of D. J. Durbin's cane were more than evident. In the afternoon I don't see how I could have missed them. I looked back at her. She seemed thinner, her cheek bones high and pale so that her eyes seemed even larger and brighter. Her lips were scarlet and unsmiling. In such almost static repose she was prettier than I'd ever thought she was. Her light hair was brushed up in curls on the top of her head, with a red bow in them matching the belt of her white dress and the red suede nonsense she had on her feet for shoes. She did look very young, and if she was going to dress up so gaily and then sit here and mope I was afraid Colonel Primrose was right in saying she would be a fool.

"Well," she said, straightening up and looking at me, "Mr. Buck brought me home last night."

It was an abrupt out-of-the-blue statement. Whether she realized its implications or not I didn't know.

"Which means Colonel Primrose knows it now," I said. "Has he been here yet?"

She shook her head.

102

"Mr. Buck was sweet," she went on. "We stayed out in the car and talked a long time. He said I didn't have to worry about . . . about Cass and . . . Courtney, even if Mr. Durbin is dead and she has a lot of money, because . . . he says Cass isn't that kind of a person."

"Oh, dear," I said. It was out before I realized it. One of the axioms of Colonel Primrose's procedure is that if he can find out who Sergeant Buck and I think is innocent, he can then and there signal to the hangman to make ready.

She looked at me, her face blank and immobile.

"Why? Is he always wrong?"

I didn't like to say, "Well, he's not always right." In fact there was very little I could say.

"He's wrong this time, anyway," she went on.

"You're sure, darling?" I asked.

She nodded.

"You know I said I didn't want anybody to feel sorry for me, Grace. And I still don't. I think it's really wonderful that . . . that now she's free and she's got everything and they can begin all over again. Not many people have a second chance until they're too old to care. And all this sort of thing . . ."

She looked around at the paint job she'd done and the simple inexpensive antiques she'd glued together and scraped and rubbed down herself, not seeing now, I suppose, the charm they really had.

". . . It simply bores the pants off Cass, and there's no reason why it shouldn't. I want him to have the other."

She got up and put the tray with her untasted breakfast on the table by the back room door.

"He's been in love with her much longer than I knew," she said calmly. "I keep feeling I've got to make you understand that I . . . I think that's important. If I loved anybody that much I'd want to be with him, and I'd get so I hated anybody who'd . . . who'd sidetracked me for very long. So I'm sort of saving myself something too."

She came over to me.

"I know Cass is in an awful spot, Grace. You don't know how bad a spot it is—and I wouldn't have if it hadn't been for Mr. Buck. People tell you the little mean things they hear but they never tell you the important big things."

There was a sudden bitterness in her eyes that I wouldn't have thought she was old enough to know.

"You see, Cass doesn't know, and it's the kind of thing I can't tell him. It's too terrible. Courtney could tell him, but I couldn't. That's why she'll always be better for him than I will."

I wasn't sure. It seemed to me that perhaps the fewer bitter

103

truths wives tell their husbands the better off they both are. It also seemed to me that this was one I could keep to myself just then.

"You see, Mr. Buck told me last night that I held Cass's future, and Courtney's, both in the hollow of my hand," she said quietly.

Hearing Sergeant Buck called "Mister" in the first place was startling enough, but hearing of him in that role was astounding. I could imagine Duleep Singh as a swami without much trouble if I had to, in fact with the mere addition of a jewelled turban. Swami Buck was a concept that was far beyond me.

Molly must have interpreted my surprise as something else.

"I wasn't coming back here when I left the Durbins' last night, Grace. I just wasn't ever coming here again. But Mr. Buck brought me here. He said if I left the house now it would make it look as if everything was . . . was true, and Cass wouldn't have a chance. He said if I didn't act like I believed in him, nobody else would either. If I wanted to go later he said I could, but right now he said I had to go around and act like I thought it was fine for Cass to stand by and help Courtney out, and not let on to anybody that I cared or was upset or hurt."

"It makes a lot of sense," I said.

There was something rather moving in the picture of the grim-visaged, fishy-eyed man sitting outside in the car, talking out of the corner of his lantern jaw, telling Molly the simple truths that probably nobody else could have made her take so like a trusting child.

"Of course he doesn't know . . . some of it," she said, looking away again. "He doesn't know why I was at the Durbins'. Or . . . about this."

She bent down and pulled a leather gladstone bag out from under the sofa, and opened it.

"When he says Cass isn't that kind of a person he doesn't understand it's just that Courtney means more to him than . . . anybody else does. Just as . . . I'll probably always mean more to Randy than anybody else.—He's been so sweet."

Her eyes softened for an instant. The smile in them faded as she turned back a narrow flap in the bottom of the bag and pulled a fastener that held it down. She lifted the flap up.

"I was unpacking his things yesterday," she said. "I shouldn't have opened this, maybe, but I'm glad I did. I . . . understand better, now."

She took out a dark green leather portfolio with a border of gold tooled leaves.

"This was my father's—I gave it to Cass."

104

She opened it. There was a picture of Courtney inside. It was an unmounted photograph, fairly large, and very lovely. Under it were five or six other pictures of her, cut from the Washington newspapers, some of them going back to the time he'd first met her about six years ago. Molly took them up and looked at them, and put them back again. There was one other picture, of another woman, that had something vaguely familiar about it.

"That's his sister, the one who died," she said. "They look a little alike, don't they, except for the coloring."

She put it down and closed the flap again.

"She and Courtney I guess are the only women he'll ever really love."

She closed the bag, pushed it back under the sofa and got up.

"I just wish he hadn't used the folder I gave him to . . . to carry them around in. That's all I really mind. It's funny, isn't it, how little things seem more important than big ones, sometimes."

She stood there looking around the room as if it had suddenly become strange and unfamiliar to her.

"Look, Molly," I said. "Why don't you come over to my house and have lunch? You oughtn't to stay here alone and think about things. It doesn't do any good."

"I know it doesn't—and thanks. But I'm going down town to lunch. I'm going with Duleep Singh."

I don't know why that disturbed me, but it did.

"You know, Grace, he's really wonderful," she said with sudden warmth. "I could fall in love with him. He understands everything without your having to tell him. And he can see my life, he said. It's like a garden . . . a flower garden in the spring. Grace, he's really wonderful."

Her eyes were shining the way they should have shone for Cass . . . or even Randy. I'm afraid as I left the house mine were dull and glazed. I was worried. I was much more worried about her now than I had been when I saw her bed was empty at three o'clock on the morning little Achille was poisoned in her house.

19

I don't know whether rumor travels faster in Washington than it does anywhere else in the world, or only seems to. Or if there really is something in the excessive humidity here that makes the dragon's tooth, once planted, grow faster than the bean stalk in the fairy tale. By the time I left the Red Cross about quarter to one, at any rate, I began to wonder whether it wouldn't be wise to go directly to the ration board and apply for enough gasoline to get me out to St. Elizabeth's for a nice quiet rest.

Of course everybody was simply goggle-eyed to begin with. And when one woman said Molly Crane was leaving town —she'd called up her daughter and asked her to substitute as nurse's aide for her that morning—it was like that spontaneous roar that goes up at the race track when they're off. Though women's tongues, and I dare say men's, can run faster than Whirlaway's backers ever hoped he could in their most sanguine moods. One woman said she'd always thought D. J. Durbin was an Axis agent, and now she was sure of it. Somebody else said Horace Blodgett had collapsed and had to be taken out, and somebody else had heard it was Courtney and not Horace. A woman I don't know said Courtney had been to the doctor's office at ten that morning and she was beaten black and blue from her head to her heels. She'd got that from the sister of a girl the receptionist had telephoned to tell about it.

Opinion seemed to be divided into two definite and mutually exclusive camps. One was that a fellow spy had done it, and the other implied rather than stated that Courtney Durbin knew a great deal more than she was telling the police. The story of Courtney and Molly's brief passage at the Abbotts' was common currency, magnified to a point unrecognizable to me. Molly was on her way to Reno and was going to marry Randy in six weeks and one day. Cass had lost his job as of that morning. I don't recall who it was who said that, but she had it straight from the Pentagon.

Those were just a few of the hush-hush bits that were going the rounds with the speed of light. I was rather surprised that no one I heard even inquired who the dinner guests were, or seemed to think it odd that they had departed silently into nowhere and hadn't turned up again.

Or that's what I'd thought about them until I went down Connecticut Avenue with three friends to have lunch in the air-cooled cocktail lounge at the Garfield Hotel. As we went in the lobby I saw Colonel Primrose standing under the clock, looking at his watch. He glanced up and smiled, and when we got to him he stopped us, and it ended with my staying to have lunch with him.

"—You'll be particularly interested," he said, after the other women had gone on in. "I'm waiting for Mr. Austin."

"Really?" I said. "Where did you find him?"

I was pretty excited, though I'd rather it had been Sondauer-Skagerlund.

"He phoned in from New York this morning," Colonel Primrose said. He smiled a little at the look on my face. "He saw about it—he says—in the papers, and he's flying down with Sondauer. I imagine he wants to see me even worse than Bigges wants to see him. And his name isn't Austin. It's Armistead. He's a member of the New York law firm of Ryan, Armistead and Meggs."

"What *is* the point of all this pseudonymity?" I asked.

Just then I spotted Mr. Armistead-Austin whipping in the door. His impeccability looked very frayed around the edges. In fact, Mr. Armistead had obviously had an extremely uncomfortable few hours and was making no attempt to disguise it. He even seemed glad I was there, to give him some kind of authentication, as he'd never met Colonel Primrose. Particularly, as he added, as nobody with any sense would believe his story, or what he'd been through since the arrival of his firm's fabulous client.

"My God, this man Sondauer's crazy as a bedbug," he said, with a passion I wouldn't have suspected he was capable of. "I *tell* you. He's like a half-witted child, with his practical jokes when he's not doing business. And when he is, My God, he makes your hair curl the other way. And this game of hide and seek. I told him this morning we can play it if that's what he wants to do, but I'm damned if we're going to be mixed up in a murder case just to amuse him."

We'd gone into the crowded lounge to the table Colonel Primrose had reserved, in the corner under the potted palms.

"And that business of the kitten," Mr. Armistead said. "He says he didn't send it, but of course he sent it. He told me he'd once got Durbin cornered in a deal by having a plank put up under the windows with some liver on it and a few cats to jump up and get it. It had Durbin in such a state he didn't know what he was doing. When he told me about it he laughed till I thought he'd break a blood vessel. Durbin was deathly afraid of them. If it hadn't been for Mrs. Durbin getting hurt last night Sondauer would have been as delighted as a child."

"It isn't just black cats, then?" I asked.

Colonel Primrose glanced at me rather oddly, I thought.

"All cats," Mr. Armistead said. "Sondauer says that's why he never goes out of the house if he can help it. It's a . . . a pychotic state. But when Durbin started thrashing that stick around it looked like homicidal mania to me. And he certainly wasn't in a state to do business afterwards. Sondauer had him there. But he didn't kill him."

"You're sure about that?" Colonel Primrose asked politely.

"My God, man!"

Mr. Armistead stared at him.

"Of course I'm sure of it. I was there all the time. That's what I'm here to tell you. The man's got a screw loose, but he's gentle as a lamb when there's no money involved. That was the whole trouble."

"Suppose you tell me about it," Colonel Primrose said equably. "Shall we order first? A martini, or a daiquiri?"

"Just a plain double rye for me," Mr. Armistead said. "And just plain water on the side."

Colonel Primrose smiled. It was a medicinal and not a social measure Mr. Armistead was taking, I supposed.

While the waiter took our order I glanced around the dimly lighted room. The tables were crowded together and all full. The harassed waiters, too few of them and some of them new to the job, were doing their best, and if it hadn't been that their best wasn't very fast I'm not sure I would have seen Molly and Duleep Singh at all. Not that they were in a hurry to be served—it was the table next to them. They were sitting side by side on a white leather seat against the wall, completely absorbed in their conversation, oblivious, apparently, to waiters and guests alike.

Oblivious also to the fact that Cass, Randy and two other Army officers were at a round table toward the center of the room. Whether Cass saw them or not I couldn't tell. His back was toward us, and if I hadn't seen Randy get up to speak to an older woman who stopped a moment at their table, I wouldn't have known they were there at all. But Randy had seen Molly and Duleep Singh. Every time I glanced up he was looking at them. His face was stormy and when the others laughed about something he didn't join in. The two sets of them—Molly and Duleep, and Randy and Cass —made a curious visual obbligato to Mr. Austin-Armistead's solo recital at our table in the corner.

"It was after you left, Mrs. Latham," he said.

I liked his describing my departure so simply.

"Durbin cancelled dinner, and Sondauer likes his food. There was a good deal of unpleasantness about Mrs. Durbin's hands. Durbin and Sondauer had words in some language. It sounded like Chinese to me, and I guess they both know it. They've been out there enough. Sondauer was still sore about it—he had tears in his eyes when she went in. He kept saying, 'That beautiful lady, those beautiful hands!' He's sentimental as mush anyway."

Mr. Armistead shook his head.

"I frankly can't make him out," he said helplessly. "He's beyond me. Anyway. We got in the library, and the man brought sandwiches and poured Scotch and sodas. Sondauer said he wouldn't eat the sandwiches, it was an insult to offer them when he expected to be fed, and he wouldn't touch the liquor because he wanted to be alive in the morning. That made Durbin sore. He picked up his cane. Sondauer made a dive for it. He's fat but he can move like a cat if he wants to. He wanted to then, and he wrenched the stick out of Durbin's hand and snapped it in two like a match. He tossed

108

it down on the desk, and they started snarling that lingo of theirs. All of a sudden Sondauer shoved his chair back and turned to me and said, 'We're going.' I was glad to."

Colonel Primrose listened intently, without, however, seeming either surprised or particularly enlightened, as far as I could tell.

"When was that?" he asked. "It didn't happen at once when you——"

"No, no. They talked quite a while first. We left about half-past eight. We got down here, and Sondauer didn't like the menu."

Mr. Armistead looked at us grimly.

"—So he said we were going to New York to get something to eat . . ."

He shook his head helplessly again.

"Just like that. He went out and phoned the maid to bring his briefcase—I had mine—while I got a sandwich. I'm not so choosy when I'm hungry. He met the girl out here on the corner, gave her five ten-dollar bills, he told me, and told her if Durbin or anybody else called to say we'd gone to Brazil. My God, I began to think he really meant to get his supper there. The idea of space isn't in the man's mind at all."

Colonel Primrose nodded absently. "They weren't quarrelling just about Mrs. Durbin's hands, I imagine," he said. "What——"

"No, I gathered Durbin was annoyed because Sondauer tried to see this young man Crane," Mr. Armistead said. "I don't know how he came in the picture. These people don't tell you any more than they have to. Durbin apparently thought Sondauer was trying to doublecross him and get some information about a deal that—I gathered—Durbin was planning to do the doublecrossing on.—We've represented some of Sondauer's interests in this country, Colonel, and expedited his people through, and so on. But this is the first time we've had to do with the big man himself—or we'd have signed off years ago."

"Sondauer didn't talk about Crane?"

"He was pretty annoyed at not knowing it was Crane on the plane with him. He learned it from a reporter coming in from the airport. No, he talked chiefly about Durbin. He's openly delighted Durbin's out of the way. It clears up a lot of his problems, it seems. But he didn't put him out of the way, Colonel. Durbin was very much alive when we left.—We got a plane at half-past nine, by a simple method. Sondauer bought two places from a couple of young Marine officers who didn't happen to be in a hurry, and paid them enough to more than have a time in New York before they went on."

Colonel Primrose was silent for a moment.

"It would probably interest Sondauer," he said then, deliberately, "to have Crane make a favorable report to the War Department? For the Monday session, say?"

Mr. Armistead looked down at the remains of his double rye for some time. He shrugged.

"Without prejudice, and distinctly off the record, it undoubtedly would interest him . . . a great deal. It wouldn't interest my firm, Colonel. Just for one thing, I've got two sons and a son-in-law in this war, and my partners have boys in it. We don't want any part of anything that isn't out in the open. If Mr. Crane is like that, at a time like this . . ."

He shrugged again.

"This business of coming down here under assumed names, and taking rooms in a private house, was very distasteful to me. Sondauer said it was a joke, and God knows it was just as funny as his others. It was something I was in before I knew anything about it, and it's something I'm out of as of this morning at nine o'clock."

Colonel Primrose nodded. "There's still something I want you to do for me," he said. "We'll go into it after lunch. You have a room here?"

"Yes."

"And Sondauer?"

Mr. Armistead nodded. "Under his own name, too," he said, with a kind of grim satisfaction.

20

Molly and Duleep Singh were still there when we got up to go. He was turned toward her on the seat, talking earnestly. She was looking in front of her with a sort of rapt, far away blindness in her eyes, a smile on her lips. If he was talking to her about the flower garden her life was to be, she was certainly seeing it as a radiant and wistful vision, the taste of ripe pomegranate seeds already in her mouth.

I saw Colonel Primrose glance toward them before he rose, and when he looked at me he smiled faintly and shook his head a little.

There were four women with enormous straw cartwheels on their heads at the table where Cass and Randy had been sitting. When they'd left I didn't know, so I'd missed the last look Randy must have shot Molly and the Indian, absorbed in their own conversation under the potted palms. Whether Cass's not going over to speak to them meant he hadn't seen them, and Randy hadn't told him they were there, or whether he wasn't interested enough to bother, or whether he was too interested, I didn't know, and with things as they were I wouldn't have hazarded a guess. Cass in the last few days had become a complete enigma to me.

He and Randy were waiting for a taxi when I came out on the street. Colonel Primrose and Mr. Austin-Armistead were inside taking the elevator when I left them, Mr. Armistead with slightly renewed jitters at the idea of an impending interview with Inspector Bigges. I envied them, because coming out into the street was like stepping from the icebox onto a sizzling platter.

"Hello there, Grace."

Cass, looking comparatively cool in a comparatively unrumpled seersucker suit, hailed me from the curb. Randy said hello grumpily. From their faces you would have thought it was his wife who was inside lunching with the fascinating Hindoo, and his head the thundercloud sat upon, ready to burst into a torrential downpour. If Cass had any idea the reverse was true, it wasn't apparent. His gray eyes were clear and steady, his manner friendly and unperturbed.

"Can we give you a lift, if and when?" he asked. "Which way you going?"

"I'm going to Courtney's," I said.

A car pulled up just then and let out more harassed-looking men with bulging briefcases and limp collars than could ever possibly have got in. Cass and Randy stemmed the tide of people waiting to take over, and because nobody else was going above Dupont Circle we had it to ourselves.

"Tell her for me, will you," Cass said as we started off, "that Julie Ross says Durbin phoned for Skagerlund, or Sondauer, whoever the hell it was, a few minutes past nine. He wanted her to have him call as soon as he came in. I don't know what it means, but Julie wanted me to tell her."

"It means one thing, anyway," Randy said shortly. "It means they weren't there and Durbin was. I don't see it helps anybody but them . . . and Bigges and the good gray Colonel. She's sure it was him? She's such a half-wit."

"She knows his voice," Cass said. "Or says so. He's called them before. I'd just as soon they were out of it, myself. It would be a bad show if the Board decides to okay Sondauer's scheme."

I felt my heart sink a little. "Are they likely to?" I asked.

He shrugged.

"You can't tell. It depends on the stockpile. We may need his . . . what he's got bad enough to go along with him. There might be political reasons—or State reasons—for doing it that are out of my bailiwick. It isn't as simple as it looks."

The taxi made a U-turn on Massachusetts Avenue, and drew up in front of the iron gate.

"You're not coming in?" I asked.

111

Cass hesitated. "Tell her I'll see her later," he said. "I'll be at the office. She'll know."

I got out of the cab.

"Oh, and look, Grace," he said. It had started up, and stopped. He leaned out the window, lowering his voice. "Tell her I talked to Blodgett, and no soap. Goodbye."

Flowers, still wilted, opened the door. A detective was sprawled in a chair in the library playing the radio. I've never seen anyone look quite as bored. His face lighted as I came in, and fell as instantly.

"I got to take your name, miss," he said without enthusiasm. "I'm getting tired sitting around here doing nothing."

Courtney looked as if she felt the same way. She was dressed and sitting on a stool in front of the fireplace, going through a lot of old letters piled on a table. She looked bored but fairly calm. Her hands were more elaborately taped and the fingers swollen, but she could still use them.

"Just badly bruised," she said. "I can't hold anything heavy or do anything much, but at least there aren't any bones broken. They took an X-ray this morning. Lord, I'm fed up with all this. I wish they'd let me out of here. I suppose I could go somewhere where I wouldn't have to pretend I'm a sorrowing widow for a while. Sit down, angel."

She smiled a little. "I'm glad you came."

"I just saw Cass," I said.

Her face brightened and she looked at me expectantly. I thought it was the most revealing single gesture indicating the status quo that anybody had so far made.

"He said to tell you . . . there were three things," I said. "First, Julie talked to Mr. Durbin a few minutes past nine . . . your guests left about half-past eight. Second, Horace says no soap, and third, Cass'll see you later."

Her face was a curiously changing mirror at each one of them. She seemed bewildered at the first, annoyed at the second and not as happy at the third as could be expected, obviously wishing the later were sooner.

"—Thanks," she said after a moment. She sat quietly a while.

"I hoped Mr. Blodgett would take over my affairs for me," she said then. "Oh, well, he's too much of an old fogy anyway. But I don't see that it helps anything to know he phoned Julie then. In fact, it . . . it isn't possible."

"Why not?"

"Because it isn't," she said coolly. "Inspector Bigges was here this morning. Back at the beginning again. They're sure he was . . . dead by a little after eight at the latest."

I stared at her, I suppose open-mouthed.

She shivered a little.

"—Rigor had begun to set in by the time they got him

112

to the . . . hospital, or wherever it was. I don't know about that sort of thing, but Inspector Bigges is positive about it."

She looked away. "It's . . . all pretty horrible."

"If you only hadn't broken up the records," I said tentatively.

"I know." Her voice was unsteady. "If I'd had time to put them on and see. But . . . I didn't. I couldn't be sure, and it seemed better not to take a chance. If I'd known he was dead around eight o'clock . . . But it's done, and it's spilt milk. You see, Cass was here after eight."

My mind was in pretty much of a whirl, but even then I'd supposed already that that must be it, and was also the reason for Molly Crane's activity. But it wasn't the sort of thing I could have said to her in so many words.

"It was my fault," she went on, her eyes fixed down into the fireplace. "I was almost out of my mind when I came upstairs. I called him up and he came over. He came in the back way, because . . . well, he didn't want D. J. to see him —for several reasons. I was in an awful state. My hands hurt like fury and everything had just seemed so gone to hell I couldn't bear it. He was terribly angry, of course. He wanted to go down and see D. J., and . . . I don't know . . . I thought he had. And that . . . that's what had happened. But . . . he was already dead.—I haven't seen him since Inspector Bigges told me."

We sat there in two separate pools of silence for a few moments. She got up, went over to the window and stood looking out for a long time, it seemed to me. She turned back at last.

"Do you think Molly will give him up without . . . without a lot of . . . trouble?" she asked, with what seemed to me no more than a decent amount of reasonable hesitation.

"I don't know, darling," I said. "What does he think?"

"We haven't talked about it. We couldn't very well with policemen listening at the key holes. They've cleared me of actual physical complicity, on account of my hands. Inspector Bigges told me this morning he'd thought I might have . . . done it, but the doctor told him I couldn't. Which is sweet of all of them. My God, as if I'd *murder* anybody, no matter how much I might have . . . wanted to. It's so silly."

She came back and sat down again.

"I don't know what he'd think if he knew Cass had been in the house."

"I'll bet I do," I said.

"Well, so do I."

After a long silence she said, "You know, it's funny. I wanted money, and now I've got it. But if the people you like, and respect, like—well, like Horace Blodgett—are going to act as if I didn't have any right to it, or got it some way

113

I shouldn't, that'll leave just the people who think you're swell just because you've got money, no matter where or how. . . . And . . . well, I'd hate that . . . kind of a life."

She moved abruptly.

"Anyway, let's not talk about it any more. It's driving me nuts. Your Colonel was here this morning too. He's taken away all the records, out of the vault in the cellar. God knows what's in them and what he's going to hear. I keep trying to remember things I've said going through there. The thing was always on, so he'd know when anyone else was in there. He was so strange. He must have had a very restless and unhappy soul—he was suspicious of everybody. People can't *live* that way. But let's not talk about it. Where did you have lunch?"

I could tell her where but not who with if she wanted to get off the subject, so I told her at the Garfield and about the four women with the cartwheel hats, and about four o'clock I left. The attempt at other conversation had been pretty futile. It was like having a gaunt, grim and terrible spectre draped in black sitting on the parlor sofa while a tea party's going on, with everybody trying to pretend it wasn't sitting there. It was in Courtney's shell-pink room all the time I was. It had been there before I came, and I knew when I went I'd left her alone with it.

I'd been standing a few moments on the curb, trying to decide whether to walk or attempt the bus, when a large car drew up and stopped. Duleep Singh was in the back preparing to get out when he saw me.

"How do you do, Mrs. Latham?"

He took off his hat, got out and bowed.

"Are you leaving?" he asked.

I nodded.

"Then let me take you where you are going. It's a little early anyway, I'm afraid."

He glanced up at the house, and looked back at me. I wondered whether he was again seeing the black wall with nothing beyond it, which was rather the way I felt at the moment, or whether the sombre examining interest in his eyes was something I was imagining.

"I'd be delighted," I said.

We got in the car. He gave the driver my address with a readiness that surprised me, not knowing he knew it. He'd been there only once, largely because Lilac has strong prejudices about what Shakespeare's Prince of Morocco called the shadowed livery of the burnished sun and it's too difficult to try to educate her.

"How is Mrs. Durbin?" he asked with great kindness.

"She's bearing up, I guess," I said, with rather less.

Seeing Duleep Singh had brought that question of hers

114

about Molly back into my mind, and I found myself getting unreasonably annoyed at her, in a sort of delayed reaction. It was probably standing out in the heat that did it.

"She's an unhappy woman," he said.

That annoyed me a little too—this whipping out of the crystal ball at the drop of a hat.

"Yes, she told me you said there was a black wall in front of her," I said. "I didn't know you were a mystic."

"I'm not," he said equably. "But people fascinate me. And I believe they make their own lives by their desires."

He smiled.

"I'll admit I'm a charlatan, if you like, Mrs. Latham. And like all charlatans, knowing more of certain people's background than they know I know, I surprise them, and from then on they're highly receptive."

He smiled again.

"It's amusing to have people assume that because you came from a certain country you must therefore have a special knowledge of the human soul. I find it a great social asset —in a country where women are dominant children."

"It doesn't occur to you that you might do considerable harm?" I asked.

His face sobered instantly.

"On the contrary."

He looked at me thoughtfully.

"I have known a good deal about D. J. Durbin, for the last ten years . . . longer, in fact. I've seen him ruin other women's lives, and throw them out, old and afraid, when they should just begin to live."

He spoke with a subdued passion that was rather alarming, he was ordinarily so polished and urbane.

"He had some extraordinary fascination for women. I don't know what it was. But it was hypnotic. Even after his accident he had it, and no matter how cruel he was to them they still crawled to him. And he hated them. When I told Mrs. Durbin there was nothing but a black wall in front of her, I meant it. She wasn't in love with him . . . then. Some time she would have been. As long as she resisted it because of her love for someone else she was safe. But that wouldn't have lasted. Durbin loved the chase, and had all too little of it. To that degree she fascinated him. She knew, when we talked that evening, that she was facing a wall. I told her nothing she didn't know herself. In fact, she told me before I told her."

"And . . . Mrs. Crane?" I asked. "Did she tell you she knew there was a garden of flowers . . ."

I said it before I really realized what a dreadful thing I was doing. He looked at me with a smile, however, neither annoyed nor embarrassed. Still he didn't answer right away.

I let it go, and didn't try to finish or undo what I'd said, knowing from long experience how futile it is.

"Perhaps I shouldn't have denied being a mystic," he said at last. "I can see the inner light that shines from Mrs. Crane. She is of the pure of heart. She has wisdom, and she has faith. If circumstance clouds it momentarily, she will come out richer in wisdom, and still pure of heart. Nothing will spoil her, nothing tarnish her. She will always find happiness, because happiness is in one's self, Mrs. Latham. It will be wherever she is, because she will take it with her. Mrs. Durbin will never find it, because wherever she goes she must also take herself."

He turned and looked at me.

"That is my sincere belief. If telling her that, when she needs confidence in herself and in her own standards, is the trick of a charlatan, then I am a base one indeed."

♦

21

It wasn't until after I'd gone in the house and Duleep Singh had gone back to Courtney's house that I began to be disturbed about him again. Just because the future may be going to be a garden of flowers doesn't mean there isn't a rocky road on the way to it, especially if one is only twenty-two. It was interesting that Colonel Primrose thought Molly would be a fool while Duleep Singh had so much faith in her wisdom. It may have been their different points of view, I thought. All I could see of her wisdom now seemed to come from Sergeant Buck. I found myself wondering whether he'd told the Colonel about her. But I didn't have to wonder long.

Lilac came heavily up the stairs from the kitchen as I went into the garden sitting room.

"Mis' Grace, the Sergeant was over here this mornin'," she said.

The armed truce that exists between them seemed momentarily less armed.

"He says please to tell you, what th' Colonel don' know, don' hurt him. But I say, I 'spec' you know that bettern' what he does."

She hadn't got back downstairs again before the door bell rang, and to keep her from having to plod up I went out to answer it. It was Horace Blodgett. If it had been the Bey of Algiers I wouldn't have been any more surprised. Horace isn't an afternoon caller. In fact he'd never been at the house, before six and without Corinne, in all the years he'd been coming there to see me and my parents before me.

"Come in," I said. "How nice . . . or is it?"

I had a sudden sinking feeling he'd come to tell me my affairs were in such a state I'd have to find myself a government job.

"It will be for me," he said, putting his hat and briefcase on the table. "I allowed myself time to miss a bus and get out here by five-thirty. I made it in five minutes, and that ancient skeletal formation at the Colonel's won't let me in until he gets home."

That was Lafayette, Colonel Primrose's house man, who's been there almost as long as the house has.

"So I thought perhaps you'd take me in until it's time. It's pretty hot, walking the streets."

We went back to the sitting room, and I poured him a glass of sherry.

"He wants me to officiate at some affair he's fixed up," he said, sniffing cautiously at it. "I take it he wants counsel."

"I imagine 'he' is Mr. Austin-Armistead."

"Yes, he told me."

He chuckled dryly.

"Under the seal of confidence, unfortunately. It's a story I would like to be able to tell. I can see Armistead. He's one of the most meticulously conscientious persons I know."

"You're pretty meticulous yourself, aren't you?" I said. "Courtney's distressed that you won't take over her affairs."

He shook his head. " 'Fastidious' is a better word. I'd made my position clear."

He sipped his sherry, which relieved me a little. Heaven knows it cost enough to be good.

"What about Mr. Armistead, Horace?" I asked. "Is he as dependable as he sounds? It's all very mixed up. He says they left around half-past eight, with Mr. Durbin very much alive. Inspector Bigges——"

"If Armistead says that, I would depend on it," Horace said. "I've known him for years. What about Bigges?"

"Courtney says he says it can't be true. Durbin must have been dead around eight o'clock, from the autopsy. And yet Julie Ross says he called her after nine."

He smiled at what I suppose was the totally uncomprehending look on my face.

"A reputable lawyer has what must seem to the layman a naive veneration for the courts. Murder is a serious thing. If Sondauer had killed Durbin, Armistead couldn't afford to be a party to concealment. Moreover, he would never have thought of it. He'd have called a first-rate criminal lawyer first, and the police second, and tried his best to get his client off. He wouldn't have cut and run."

He gave me a sort of wintery half-smile.

"You must consider another point. A lawyer lives by litigation. He isn't interested in having litigants die, especially

117

large ones. It's most painful to him—unless he is to settle the estate, of course."

He changed the subject abruptly. "—My chief concern I'm afraid isn't Durbin. It's Cass and Molly, Grace. I don't like to see him in the position he's in, and I'm concerned about her. I saw her with Duleep Singh today. I don't mean to suggest I don't think he's an honorable man. But he's too attractive and . . . sympathetic, let's say. And at the moment Molly is highly vulnerable."

"I know," I said. "It disturbs me too. So do Courtney and Cass, frankly."

Horace shook his head.

"I have confidence in Cass. I think he's being exceptionally blind. I told him so today, as a matter of fact, and he told me politely to mind my own business. Which of course he had every right to do. I don't know how serious his affair with Courtney was. She was, and I expect is, in love with him—and she's a shrewd and calculating woman."

"I don't know either," I said. "He has a whole stack of pictures of her, in a portfolio in his suitcase. Poor Molly found them. She showed them to me this morning. She certainly doesn't think he's forgotten. And he's been over at Courtney's a lot. He was there this morning."

"I'm sorry," Horace said. "I wish she'd married Randy, and I told her so when she told me she was going to take Cass."

He shrugged.

"Youth is quixotic, and I suppose I'm getting very old. I understand Randy poked somebody in the nose this morning for suggesting Cass was feathering his own nest."

He shook his head and looked at his watch. "I must go," he said, getting up. "I don't like this business very much."

I followed him to the door and gave him his hat and briefcase. He stepped outside, hesitated and turned back.

"Actually, Grace," he said, "the reason I came is that I'd like you to look in on Corinne, some time when you're over our way. She was pretty much upset last night, the way her swami walked out on her. I think she was hoping for a quiet mystical chat, and she insists he was out of the house before we were."

He smiled the way one does at the antics of a wayward and unpredictable child, and went down the stairs.

Colonel Primrose was just getting out of a taxi in front of his house. He waved to me and walked up to meet Horace, and they went back together.

I felt rather sorry for Cass Crane as I went back inside. I'd seen Colonel Primrose rig up his so-called traps to clear people before, but I'd never seen anybody come out of them except bound hand and foot with the shadow of the iron bars already falling across them. I found myself hoping it would be Randy and not Duleep Singh whose star was in the ascendant.

It was ten o'clock Saturday morning when Colonel Primrose came over to my house. Molly was coming in later—he'd phoned me to ask her to. He looked very tired, as if the heat had got him completely down and he hadn't had any sleep for days.

He had a clothbound record book under his arm, which he put down on the table.

"I haven't a phonograph at my place," he said. "I thought you'd be interested, and I'd rather Molly would come here than go . . . anywhere else."

Whether he meant to the Department of Justice, or War, or simply to Headquarters, I didn't know and thought it better not to ask. He opened the top of the phonograph and started to take a record out of the book. As he did the doorbell rang. He closed the book and looked around.

"That's probably Bigges," he said with a noticeable lack of enthusiasm. "I left word I'd be here. I didn't expect him till later."

It was Inspector Bigges, and he didn't look any fitter than the Colonel. He came in, said "Hot, isn't it," cast a professional glance around—it was just force of habit, I suppose, but it made me feel a little uncomfortable—sat down and put his hat under his chair. He seemed to think that was the safest place for it. I wasn't so sure, the way Sheila kept smelling at it.

"Well, those records of Durbin's, Colonel," he said. "I've been through the lot of 'em. Here's a list of all the people who come in the picture at all who were on the place that night."

He took a slip of paper out of his pocket and put on his horn-rimmed spectacles.

"I've sort of divided them into three groups. First the ones we heard talk, on those records, before Thursday night. It just means they'd been in the place themselves, any time before. You remember the records break off where Durbin invited Sondauer and Armistead to dinner. Here it is.

"Mrs. Durbin.

"Mrs. Latham."

He looked over his glasses at me.

"That's you. The Colonel and I were saying you had the best voice of the lot. It's low, like. You ought to go on the radio."

What on earth it was I'd said, some time heaven knows how far back, in D. J. Durbin's library he didn't go into, and Colonel Primrose only smiled.

"Cass Crane. Before he went away on this last trip.

"Duleep Singh.

"Sondauer.

"Armistead.

"That's the lot we know were in that room before the night he was killed, at one time or another. Then you can put in the little driver, Achille, and Flowers. There aren't any others. Achille's dead, and Flowers . . ."

He went on without bothering to explain why Flowers needn't be worried about.

"Then there's what you could call a group known to be there Thursday night who hadn't been in the place before. That's Mr. Blodgett. Also the kid that brought the kitten. I mean, we know they were there, and their voices aren't in the records.

"The third group is people whose names are mentioned in the records but aren't known to have been in the library. That's Mr. Blodgett, and Mrs. Crane."

I suppose I must have had some kind of look on my face.

"I don't mean Mrs. Crane was there Thursday night," Inspector Bigges explained. "She's connected, and her name came on the records . . . mostly with Mrs. Durbin saying what she thought of her. Mr. Blodgett's name comes in with Durbin telling Armistead that Blodgett was representing Duleep Singh in some deal and it was too bad he wasn't representing them instead of Armistead, because he was a better lawyer. The guy was sure polite. It's funny hearing Armistead say he'd be more than happy to retire and let them get Mr. Blodgett. I'll bet he meant it, from what he says."

"Have you people been listening to all those records?" I asked.

Colonel Primrose drew a long breath. "Ever since the Durbins took the house. If you're interested in the way things are done behind the scenes, it's fascinating but . . . exhausting."

"And it doesn't help much," Bigges added. "The people you'd think had the most reason to kill the man are in Chungking, or Rio, or somewhere. They weren't in Washington Thursday night when the job was done, as far as we can find."

He wiped off his perspiring forehead with the sleeve of his seersucker suit.

"Mrs. Ross insists Durbin called her house a little after nine. She's positive it was him. That bears out Armistead's statement he was alive when they left. This timing is driving me crazy, Colonel. The medicos swore at first he must have been dead at eight o'clock, or thereabouts. Rigor had begun to set in already, when they did the autopsy. He was in pretty normal shape, except he'd picked up dysentery. He'd lived in the tropics a long time. But I'm inclined to believe Armistead."

It flashed instantaneously into my mind, just then, that there was something none of them, so far as I knew, had said anything about. But I was a little startled to hear my own voice, as I hadn't meant to say what I was thinking.

"—How long does it take to get from the Garfield to the Durbins'?"

"It all depends," Inspector Bigges said. "Why?"

I could feel rather than see Colonel Primrose's black eyes snapping at me suddenly from across the room.

"I . . . was just wondering," I said hastily. "It hasn't anything to do with this."

"Oh," Inspector Bigges said. His intonation fully implied it was the kind of interruption you could expect from a woman.

"Well, we go back to the poisoning of the little driver," he went on, not very cheerfully. "And we've got to find out who got to Durbin's place just before you got there Thursday night, Colonel. And how they got in and out."

"The little driver," Colonel Primrose said very placidly, "was quite accidentally killed by D. J. Durbin, who was trying to poison Cass Crane. There's never been the slightest doubt about it, Bigges. It looks too obvious the way it happened. It wouldn't have if the little man hadn't drunk the liquor and Crane had, and Durbin had whipped off with the balance of it, which of course is what he went there to do. Durbin was well used to taking chances, through a ruthless, treacherous and damned rotten career. He got away with everything, by and large, until . . . Thursday instant. The exact time being, I take it, unknown to us. No, you can forget about Achille. The poisoner doesn't strangle people."

"All right, Colonel," Inspector Bigges said shortly. "That leaves us like this. Two doctors are ready to swear Mrs. Durbin couldn't physically have done it. We know he was dead at nine-forty or thereabouts. Armistead says he was alive at eight-thirty. The doctors say he ought to have been dead at eight. But you can't put the time of death within an hour. I'm banking on Armistead—Mr. Blodgett says he's a well-known lawyer of fine reputation. And that gives him and the multi-millionnaire clown an out."

He looked at Colonel Primrose steadily.

"My guess, Colonel, is that the person who came in that house after eight-thirty and before you people got there, and killed him, was somebody who just hated him.—Just couldn't stand it to have him alive any longer."

"That would be . . . just about my guess too," Colonel Primrose said quietly.

"All right.—Why did Mrs. Durbin break up the records?"

"The only assumption is that she knew—or thought she knew—who the murderer was," Colonel Primrose said. "And didn't want him caught."

"—The chief fellow she wouldn't want caught being the guy Durbin had tried to poison the night before."

Colonel Primrose said nothing.

"You can't get away from Cass Crane, Colonel," Bigges said doggedly. "Now I'm going to make a guess here.—Mrs. Durbin called him up after she went upstairs, all right. But she'd also called him up right after Durbin had smashed her with the stick . . . and she told him about it. Wouldn't any red-blooded fellow——"

He stopped as the doorbell sounded.

"That's Mrs. Crane, I expect," Colonel Primrose said. "She's about due now. Perhaps she can tell us something. Will you let her in?"

That was to Inspector Bigges, and it was to stop me. I sat down again.

"I've had trouble with Buck this morning, Mrs. Latham," he said, smiling a little. "You two are going to do a lot of damage, some day."

He turned to Molly as she came in. Her head was high, but her face was a little pale, as well it might have been, of course, meeting Inspector Bigges at my door. She looked quickly at me, and at Colonel Primrose.

22

Molly Crane stood there just inside the doorway.

"You wanted to see me?"

"Yes," Colonel Primrose said. "I want you to listen to . . . something I have here, and I want you to tell me something."

He hesitated for a moment.

"There was some question," he said deliberately, "about the purpose of Cass's visit to the Durbins the night he came home. And there had been some questions before that."

"Yes. That's true."

Her voice was perfectly steady.

Colonel Primrose took a record out of the book he'd brought and put it on the victrola.

"I have a conversation here between Cass and Sondauer," he said soberly. "He went to Sondauer's apartment at the Garfield last night at ten o'clock. It took us all evening to rig up Durbin's recording machine in the next room. The first voice you hear is Armistead's, Sondauer's attorney. The third is Sondauer."

He waited until the automatic needle moved over and set itself down on the black disc.

It was the most extraordinary thing to hear. Listening to Mr. Austin-Armistead I could have thought myself in the room.

"Good evening, Crane. You know Mr. Sondauer, don't you?"

"Yes, I know him. Good evening."

Then Mr. Sondauer's voice, cordial and rich, with a slightly foreign accent, though what accent it was, any more than what part of the world it was one had heard in D. J. Durbin's voice, I couldn't tell.

"We meet again, Crane. You should have told me on the plane who you were. Come, sit down. Have a drink. What will you have, Mr. Crane?"

"I won't have anything, thanks, Sondauer."

I could see Cass Crane's one eyebrow slightly raised, and the sardonic grin at one corner of his mouth.

"Mr. Blodgett told me you wanted to see me, Mr. Armistead, about getting word to your son in Africa. He didn't say Sondauer was here. If you don't mind, I think I'll go downstairs and have my drink."

"Now, come, Mr. Crane. We have a little business to talk, you and me?"

"No. We haven't, Sondauer. I'd like to tell you just what I told your rat-faced pal Durbin the other night. When I want to change my job I'll do it. We've got nice clean sewers right here in Washington. I don't have to get in yours. And don't bother to send me a bottle of poisoned Scotch the way your friend did. I can still afford to buy my own liquor. Good night."

I heard the door bang, and there was a moment's silence. Then Mr. Sondauer's voice again, slightly puzzled.

"But why did you think he would *talk* business, my friend Armistead? If he would have talked, he would not have kept quiet on the plane who he was. And Durbin has already said it was impossible."

"—I thought he might have come around."

"Ah, but he now can marry Durb——"

123

I'm sure Colonel Primrose had intended to pick up the needle arm before it got to that point. Or maybe he hadn't. At any rate, as he got it off it fairly screeched the word "marry" at us.

Molly Crane stood there, her face paler still and her amber eyes wider.

"If you played that, Colonel Primrose," she said quietly, before anyone else spoke, "to show me Cass is an honest man, you didn't have to bother. I knew that. I knew the things people said were false. I've never doubted him even for an instant."

I didn't doubt her, not for one half instant.

"And if you wanted to tell me that now he can marry Mr. Durbin's widow, you needn't have done that either, because I know that too."

She looked steadily from Colonel Primrose to the Inspector.

"And if you think he killed Mr. Durbin so he could marry her, you're very wrong."

She drew in a deep breath and let it out slowly before she went on.

"I should have told you, I guess, that I was at the Durbins' Thursday night. Mrs. Durbin called him up about a quarter past eight, as he was leaving for the Pentagon. He didn't say he was going to her house, but I knew he was. I don't know what happened to me, but I was . . . I suppose I was jealous and a fool. I was frightened, too—I didn't want him to go there after what had happened at our house. I didn't know whether Mr. Durbin was making her call just to get him there, to try to trap him . . . the way Colonel Primrose tried to."

A spot of color flared up along her high cheek bones, and she glanced across the room at him with withering angry contempt.

"I don't know what I thought I could do, but I had to go. So I followed him. He went in the back way, and so did I. Then I followed him upstairs. It's a big house, of course, and I know it better than he does, because I had friends who used to live there. She was crying, saying something about her hands, and a stick, and he was angry. Of course, anyone would be!"

She looked from one to the other of them, the color still burning in her cheeks, her voice passionate with her conviction of truth.

"I was afraid he might do something to Mr. Durbin, and I wanted to stop him. I got downstairs and waited in the drawing room. I didn't want him to know I was there unless he had to know—he'd have hated me. I hid behind the curtains and waited. Then two men came out of the library, slammed the door and went out at the front. Finally Cass came. He just came down the stairs, swearing, and went out the back way. He didn't go near the library. I waited a minute and started to go too. But the phone rang and Flowers came up and answered it. It was a friend of his, and he talked and he talked and he talked."

She moved her hands helplessly.

"It was a woman, and he told her about not having dinner and the kitten and Courtney's hands, until I thought I'd scream. I went down into the cellar. I thought I could get out that way. But I couldn't, and I came up again. It was too late then. You were there, Colonel Primrose. I could hear your voices. And Flowers was sitting out on the back step with the door open. I took my shoes off and got up the back stairs, thinking I'd ring for him and perhaps he'd go around trying to see who did it and I could get away. But then you rang for him and he was right in the hall and the drawing room, so I just stayed until . . . until I got out. It didn't matter, because I knew Cass was safe."

She turned back to Colonel Primrose.

"You see, none of you understand. You think Cass will marry Courtney because she has so much money. But that isn't fair. It won't be because of that. It's because they're in love with each other, and they both made a mistake, and they know it, now. People don't always know things till they've been through some kind of a tragedy to learn. I understand how they feel. I seem to be the only one who does."

I saw that Colonel Primrose had quietly taken another record from his book, and had glanced at the victrola. He was starting to put it on, but he stopped, looked at her soberly for a moment, and put it back in the book.

"Is he free of the suspicion you had against him, Colonel Primrose?" she asked simply.

"It wasn't my suspicion," he answered, just as simply. "But he is free of it."

She turned to Inspector Bigges. "You don't think he murdered Mr. Durbin, now?"

He looked at her and shook his head slowly.

"No. I believe your story. He'd have had to climb the garden wall to get in the library by way of the terrace, which can't be done, and the door's the only other way in. You didn't hear anybody else come in?"

She shook her head. "But I couldn't have, except when I was in the drawing room. And . . . if it's all right for me to . . . to go, somewhere else, now . . . I couldn't, while he was . . . in danger. But I'd like to give them a chance to begin without—without Cass's having to worry about hurting me. And I'd like to go home now, if I may?"

Colonel Primrose nodded, and she left quickly, the tears, I think, not as far away as she was trying to make out.

We sat there silently for a while.

"Well," Inspector Bigges said then, "no matter what the facts are, she'd only have to tell that story to a jury once. Crane's a damned fool, chucking that girl for Mrs. Durbin . . . Mrs. Durbin and all the money in creation."

It was the next morning, Sunday, that I took Sheila out for a run down the parkway above Rock Creek Drive. It was about eleven when I got back to the end of Beall Street and stopped in to see if one or both of them would like to come over for lunch, a vegetarian friend having—illegally perhaps —sent me a ham.

Cass opened the door.

"Hello, Grace, come on in," he said. He grinned without any amusement. "I know I look like I'd been on a three-weeks' bender."

I must have looked as shocked as I was. He was haggard and drawn, his eyes bloodshot and his hair a mess, and he hadn't shaved.

"Come on in, anyway," he said.

I followed him into the front room.

"Where's Molly?"

The house seemed quiet and dead. It had the curious atmosphere of a house not lived in, or one that's had something happen in it, as if the soul had been driven out for the time.

"She's at the hospital pinch-hitting for somebody."

He said it as if everything inside him was gall and wormwood.

"Sit down," he said.

"What *is* the matter, Cass?" I asked.

"Everything," he said evenly. "She's not coming back."

He pulled a battered pack of cigarettes out of his pocket. The ashtray on the arm of his chair was filled with half-smoked butts and there were two empty crumpled packages in the fireplace.

"I don't blame her. But I wish to God I hadn't left her to find out she'd made a mistake. If I hadn't gone off in a week after we were married, maybe she'd still care something about me. I guess it's my fault. But . . . gosh!"

He ran his fingers through his hair and shook his head. Then he looked up at me.

"Were you ever in love, Grace?"

"I guess so," I said.

"Not if you just guess so. Down there I couldn't sleep, I couldn't eat. She was everywhere I'd look. All the time I was away. I'd write her the sappiest letters, and then I wouldn't send them, thinking I was coming back and I'd see her. And

126

most of the time I couldn't let anybody know where I was anyway. You know, I damn near cried when I got off the plane and she wasn't there."

My face as I stared at him must have been a sheer blank. "When Courtney said she was with Randy . . . he's a swell guy. It didn't occur to me they wouldn't show up, so I insisted on waiting around, like a bloody fool, until Courtney told me they weren't coming. I still thought . . . oh, well. I didn't get on to it until she wasn't here and he said she was over at your place. Then all this ruckus comes up. I knew Durbin was out to get me, one way or another. They pulled a lot of fast ones while I was down there. Somebody on my trail everywhere I went. I'd have to fall over a gal every night to get in my room and lock the door. I didn't dare take a drink at a bar even. Well, that was okay down there, because she was here. But it isn't okay here. However. If she's in love with Randy . . ."

"Oh, for heaven's sake, Cass!" I said. "You make me *sick!*"

He stared at me as if I'd slapped his face.

"Don't you know that everybody in town thinks you're in love with Courtney—including Molly—and now that Courtney's free . . . oh, don't be an absolute *dope!*"

He stared at me still, the look on his face changing to as extraordinary a one as I've ever seen.

"—Molly knows I'm not in love with Courtney," he said, very slowly, as if not really believing I could have said what I did. "I've never been in love with her. I had no idea what . . . what it was, till I met Molly. If I'd wanted to marry Courtney I'd have done it years ago. I like her, but I wouldn't be married to her. I want to be able to come home and not have to get in a dinner jacket every night and entertain some guy because he's useful to my career. It would drive me nuts. I'm going to get along all right without a lot of money and bootlicking the right people."

He jerked his cigarette into the fireplace.

"I wouldn't have married Courtney when she was still human. Now she's got all that money . . ."

He shook his head. "You wouldn't want to feel you'd got where you were because you had a rich wife to support an embassy, or something. You see too much of that. Anyway, the point is, it's Molly, Grace. I couldn't ever love anybody else. That's just the way it is."

"And . . . you haven't told her any of this, Cass—have you?" I asked, after a minute.

"How could I?" he said. "I don't want her to feel sorry for me."

I just went out to the bar to get some ice and soda water. It was too hot to drink anything else or I'd have done it. And out there I stopped suddenly, looking at the desk. It was a mild shambles. He'd come along after me, and nodded as I looked around at him.

"—Another visitor. You know, you'd think people like Durbin and Sondauer would know you wouldn't leave information lying around. But first one, then the other. They must figure I'm so dumb that I'm beginning to think they're right."

I looked back at the litter. "Did they take anything?"

"I don't even know what was in there. Some pictures of Courtney are gone, and they're welcome to them. They've served their purpose."

They'd certainly served one that I knew of, I thought.

"That's how I found out Durbin was the nigger in the stockpile," he said. "I took 'em from his house on a hacienda up in the mountains where the airport project was. His boys down there must have let him know they'd gone, and I guess he figured I'd got them. I don't know whether he fell in love with her picture or figured when he came to Washington she'd be social and prominent enough to make his money go farthest buying up big names. He took a Washington paper, and he must have cut her out every time she appeared for about five years. He even sent to a photographer here and bought regular photographs. They didn't like to admit they'd sold them, but they did finally. I wouldn't have connected Durbin with the business if it hadn't been for them. And if Sondauer wants them, that's okay."

He stopped and looked at me suddenly.

"Maybe he's in love with her too. Well, well—Courtney, the multimillionnaires' pin-up girl."

He grinned at me for an instant.

"Well, the hell with it," he said then. "Don't tell the Colonel. I'm sick of all the cops and robbers stuff. If there's anything in the damn place anybody wants they're welcome to it."

He grinned at me again, a lopsided, twisted grin.

"You know that poem of Browning's—The Last Ride Together? 'As for me, I ride.' Well, Molly and I were taking our last ride together. In a bus, coming home from dinner at the Blodgetts'. I guess I'll always see those two, standing in the door together saying goodbye. I was thinking, what's old Horace got that I haven't got? His wife's still in love with him, and look at me. My wife says, 'It's wonderful, dear—I hope we'll still be friends.' "

"Oh, rot," I said. "Why don't you pull yourself together and do something about it. Molly's probably feeling exactly the same way."

He just shook his head. "You don't know Molly. She's wonderful, when she opens up her heart and . . . and gives it to you. If you tried to take it all you'd get would be a frozen

128

rock. I know—I tried it. She's got strength, and . . . and honor."

It's very seldom that I've put myself on the side of the angels, as it were, and feared to tread any place. I was born a rusher-in. But I had a feeling that this was very tenuous and special ground. It was something they had to understand themselves, without any well-meaning bystanders trying to explain it was all a mistake. They had to know, and not to be persuaded—otherwise there'd always be a residue of doubt in the bottom of their hearts and minds. But how they were going to know was beyond me.

23

It was still an undigested mass in the pit of my stomach and a sour-sweet taste on my tongue when Colonel Primrose came over to the house a little before three o'clock.

He looked at me with a flicker of anxiety in his eyes. "—What's the matter?"

"Nothing," I said. I smiled. "You look better than you did yesterday. Don't tell me it's all settled. Was it Sondauer or did the messenger boy turn out to be another international spider, disguised of course?"

He came on into the sitting room without saying anything. Then he said, "Why did you ask how long it takes to get from the Garfield to the Durbins'?"

"Have you ever had a sandwich at the Garfield?" I asked. He smiled a little.

"It takes anywhere up to an hour and forty minutes, these days. And Mr. Armistead said he got one, not being as choosy as——"

"Sometimes I think your I. Q. is a little higher than I've given it credit for being," he said blandly. "Or maybe it's just a low female cunning. I'm getting some advice from Horace about a . . . rather unusual legal point involved here. Do you want to come along? Buck said you could drive his car if you're out of gas. Which is practically a sign of unconditional surrender . . ."

"I'll be sure to wreck it," I said. "What's he doing?"

He chuckled.

"You'd be surprised. He's going out to get Molly at her hospital, to take her to Walter Reed. Ostensibly, she's to help cheer up an old side-kick of his. I suspect he's trying to keep her away from Singh. Buck has strong feelings about foreigners."

"Maybe he'll persuade her to go back to Cass."

"Maybe. Randy's in uniform, of course. It's hard to tell Buck anybody who's not is doing anything useful."

If I'd been driving a golden coach I couldn't have been more ill at ease than I was at the wheel of that car. Fortunately the streets were totally empty, so I couldn't have hit anything but a bus. There was one in front of me as I drove up Massachusetts Avenue, and I gave it all the room it wanted. That's how we happened to be behind it as it stopped across the street from Courtney's, and how when it started up again we saw it was Cass Crane who'd got out. He was at the iron gate—open now that there was no one inside who was afraid of retribution—by the time we went by to turn right toward the Blodgetts. The taste on my tongue was all sour, and the undigested dough in my stomach a heavier and more sodden lump.

"Well, that's the way she'll get him," I said unhappily. "Isn't there some way those two could find out for themselves that there's been a mistake? If only Molly could know Cass was bitterly disappointed she wasn't at the airport, and he could know she didn't know he was coming . . ."

I forgot all about its being Sergeant Buck's car I was driving. When I stopped in front of the Blodgetts' I was still telling him the whole business of my morning's visit, including even the cops and robbers stuff Cass had said not to tell him. It seemed so much a part of the dismal picture of the little house that I couldn't leave it out. We sat there a few minutes while I finished.

"It *is* too bad," he said, getting out. "And you're right. It's the one way Courtney can get him. The old-fashioned method's best after all . . . a knock-down drag-out row, getting everything out of your system, with a few tears before the lights go out. If Cass had only said 'Why the hell didn't you meet me?' and she'd said 'Why the hell didn't you let me know you were coming?' everything might have been fine."

He shook his head.

"Well, I always find it best to keep an ace in the hole, Mrs. Latham. We'll see."

Horace opened the door for us. Corinne, it seemed, was at a meeting about How the Power of Thought Will Silence the Guns.

"—I believe they stick thought pins in Hitler's image," Horace said with his dry smile as he led us into the air-cooled silence of the library.

"I miss her when she's out," he added. "There may be something in all this. The house is alive and sentient, if slightly crazy, when she's in it. It's curious how it draws a sane man back at the end of a day with a constant sense of anticipation, at just what new aspect of moderate lunacy will

130

meet him. We've abandoned the yellow vegetables, however, I'm glad to say. What can I do for you, John?"

"It's probably a very simple matter," Colonel Primrose said, "—about evidence. I don't know enough law to know whether I have a case or not. I thought you'd tell me."

"I know very little about criminal law," Horace said. "But there's an axiom that it is not so important for a lawyer to know the law as to know where to find the law. Perhaps we could look it up."

I looked around at the calf-lined shelves on three sides of the room. There were certainly enough books there. The portrait over the fireplace was in the only flat space not covered by them.

He turned his chair to face Colonel Primrose, and held out a box of cigars. There's something so pleasant and male and civilized about the fresh aroma of a cigar, if it's a good one.

"This concerns the Durbin case, of course," Colonel Primrose said. "In the theory of criminal detection, we say that when all possible explanations of certain sets of circumstances have to be abandoned, because they conflict with known facts, and you have only the impossible left, then your solution must lie there. What you took to be impossible was . . . not. Now I've got several impossibilities here."

He paused as if wanting to be sure he'd say it is an exact way.

"The first is Duleep Singh. I've found out quite a lot about him, going back some years. He's a man of very superior intelligence . . . and I doubt if anyone could have an intense and passionate a loathing as he had for Durbin, and with reason. But, as you know, we went from here to Durbin's house, Thursday night, and we found Durbin dead. It was impossible that Duleep Singh could have got there, and killed Durbin, before we got there.

"The next is Sondauer. Armistead, I believe, was telling the truth in saying that Durbin was alive when they left at eight-thirty. But they went down to the Garfield, Armistead got a sandwich—as Mrs. Latham has pointed out to me—and Sondauer was out of Armistead's sight, phoning Mrs. Ross's maid and waiting for her, as he said, for some twenty minutes. Barring any additional information, he could conceivably have got back to Durbin's house and killed him. Unfortunately—from one point of view—the cigar stand girl at the Garfield says he spent most of that time talking to her. It must therefore be put down as impossible that Sondauer could have returned to Durbin's house."

Horace nodded, and waited. Colonel Primrose went on deliberately.

"There is a third apparent impossibility, that seems to complicate matters a good deal. But I think perhaps I can offer a legally tenable explanation of it. Mrs. Ross claims Durbin telephoned her after nine o'clock. The police surgeons maintain he must have been dead as early as eight o'clock. Rigor had not only set in by the time they performed the autopsy, shortly after he was taken away . . . it was fairly well advanced. I'm offering two possible explanations for that, with the object of showing that the surgeons are absolutely unable to state the time of death. First: the autopsy showed that Durbin had dysentery. You remember that curiously sallow complexion of his. He probably also had malaria, and virtually all the diseases one picks up in the tropics and the Far East. But the dysentery alone would cause rigor mortis to set in with extreme rapidity.

"But another point. Rigor also sets in with extreme rapidity when people die under great emotional stress. The classic example, in all the books, is that at the battle of Antietam the bodies of soldiers were found rigid in the very act of charging over a fence, their rifles still in position. If, for example, with his curious aelurophobia, Durbin had been confronted by a cat at the time he was killed, rigor would have begun to set in almost instantaneously."

"—Is there any reason to believe he was confronted by a cat?" Horace asked.

"None at all," Colonel Primrose said.

He hesitated again for a moment.

"I think, however, that he was confronted by someone whose being there, in that way, carried with it a very powerful emotional supercharge—let's say—to his heart and brain and nervous system . . . to his whole being. I'm getting here to what I want your opinion about, because—to get back to my two impossibles again—it's precisely the effect that Duleep Singh, or Sondauer either, could have had, with their past relationships with him."

"—Have you any evidence about their past relationships with him?"

"No," Colonel Primrose said. "If there wasn't a war, Bigges could get out to Burma, China and India and spend the taxpayers' money digging them up. All the digging we can do is here at home. And that's why I've come to you."

He stopped to light his cigar again.

"I want to state a purely hypothetical case to you," he said quietly. "And I want your opinion. My guess is that what lies at the bottom of this whole business is D. J. Durbin's attitude toward . . . women. Now, Duleep Singh and Sondauer are both strongly emotional and passionate men. Let's say that one of them had a wife . . . or we'll say any woman to whom he was deeply attached, who fell in love with Durbin. And let's say that Durbin treated her with a . . . a refinement of cruelty that we as Anglo-Saxons can't understand. Suppose, for instance, that she met her death largely as a result of that cruelty."

He knocked off the small dark ash at the end of his cigar.

"Suppose he ran into Durbin in Washington here, having planned his death for . . . many years, perhaps, but never before having a chance to do anything about it—not knowing where Durbin was, perhaps, or not being able to get close to him, or perhaps again merely biding his time. Then, on Thursday, the picture suddenly changes. Durbin was about to be arrested for manslaughter and for attempted murder. It had become later than he thought. The opportunity for private . . . justice, perhaps, rather than revenge, would be gone before that night was gone.

"Well, Bigges said something with clear insight. Durbin was killed by somebody who hated him, who couldn't stand it to see him going on living any longer. And time could never be more of the essence. We were actually on our way there, Thursday night, you remember, in effect to put Durbin beyond any private reach."

"—But . . . Sondauer wouldn't know that," I said.

Colonel Primrose looked at me.

"No. He wouldn't. Duleep Singh, however, would."

"But he wouldn't," I said quickly. "Because when you said why you were going over there, when we were here Thursday night, he'd gone upstairs with Corinne, to telephone. There was only you and . . ."

I heard the sound of my voice faltering, trailing away, stopping. For a moment there was the most utter silence in that room. Colonel Primrose was looking down intently at the end of his cigar. Horace's eyes were still fixed on him, with the same focussed careful attentiveness.

I sat there blankly, the silence pounding like thunder in my ears.

24

Colonel Primrose still was silent. When Horace Blodgett spoke his voice was as calm and dry as it's always been. The gray cylinder of ash was intact on the end of his cigar, and his hands were infinitely steadier than mine. I thought there was even a kind of dry amusement, of a sort, in his eyes for an instant as Colonel Primrose looked up at him.

"—Without prejudice, John," he said, "let me take up your hypothetical case."

"That being the lawyer's way," Colonel Primrose asked

quietly, "of saying that what he is about to say cannot be used in evidence?"

Horace moved his head in assent.

"And first let me, without prejudice, put myself in the position you have . . . suggested."

He looked for one instant at that vivid lovely face smiling down at us from over the mantel.

"If the man who stole away my daughter—for instance—should ever come to Washington, I would kill him . . . and I would do it with a pleasure that it would shock you to know."

There was no change at all in his unemotional tones.

"That man did not marry my daughter, as we gave out when we returned home. But that in itself is no longer important, or reason enough in itself to kill him. Mrs. Durbin's hands were bruised when I saw her. It is an interesting thing that the man I speak of was also afraid of cats. He carried a stick too, though he was not at that time lame. When I saw my child, more than her hands were bruised, and more than her body. Her soul was more than bruised too. It was broken."

He stopped for an instant.

"My daughter was already dying when she was being taken to a hospital and the car went off the road. Fortunately, she was killed. He broke a few bones, including a hip."

The two men's eyes met steadily.

"I don't know about Duleep Singh and Durbin, John. But I rather think that if the man I'm talking about were in Washington, and over a period of time had been lulled into a feeling of security, let us say, because I had never to his knowledge seen him here, or made any attempt that he knew to communicate with him, so that he would perhaps put me down as spineless or afraid—I think if that man saw me walk into his library, he would have known at once that death was walking in with me. And I think he would be in such a state that—as you have said—rigor would set in very soon. . . ."

For a moment the room was silent again. Not one of the three of us had so much as moved.

"The man I am talking about," Horace Blodgett said steadily, "turned my daughter, in a few short years, from this . . . to this."

He pointed to the portrait over the mantel, then opened a drawer in his desk, took out a picture and handed it silently to Colonel Primrose. I looked at it across the space between us. It was the picture that had been in Cass's bag, with the pictures of Courtney. I'd thought it looked familiar to me, the morning Molly had taken them out. It was hard to see any resemblance now between this woman, who looked forty-five and was still in her early twenties when her father brought her body back to Washington, and the flame-like creature in the painting above us.

". . . In a few short years," Horace said again. "And turned my wife from a lovely, gay and happy woman into one I love perhaps even more, that I can't tell, but one who makes me want to weep as I laugh, at the courage with which she picked up the pieces of her broken heart, knowing, no matter how I tried to conceal it, that the child she worshipped was worse than dead."

He took the picture of his daughter from Colonel Primrose. He got up, went to the fireplace, struck a match and held it to one corner. As the flames stole up over the faded tragic features on the paper he dropped it onto the hearth. He watched it curl up and die, and went back to his chair.

He sat there silently for a moment, picked up his cigar and broke off the ash against the side of the tray.

"To continue our hypothetical case, John . . . again on the assumption that I should myself be in the position you've stated. If that man had come to Washington, if he had offered me, through a third party, large amounts to take his legal business, if the woman he was marrying—at last—came to me with a contract he'd so much as touched . . . I would have driven his representative and the woman out of my office. If I'd known he was about to escape me—let us say I had talked to a man he had tried to murder, and I knew that a friend was in charge of the case who seldom makes a mistake or fails to get his man—then let me tell you what I would have done.

"I would have invited a few friends to dinner . . . and on that Thursday night. I would have opened a bottle of champagne. I would have raised my glass in a silent toast to a lady I loved as dearly as a father ever loved a daughter, and again to a lady who has been child and wife and everything a man could desire. I would have repeated the profoundly solemn vow I had made to myself for both of them . . . and for myself. And after I had drunk to them, I would have gone in and eaten my yellow vegetables . . . and I would have taken the first opportunity that came to go to that man's house, and, before his wealth could perhaps subvert the law, to make him pay his debt to me. If I were fortunate, I would have found him alone in his library, where he was always to be found. I would have taken the precaution of stopping for an instant in the doorway as I went in, so that anyone who saw me might think, later, that I had then seen his dead body in his chair. It would have taken me a very short time to put an end to his horrible life . . . and to explain that time, I would have taken with me from this house a paper that I would have said I was hunting for in his room."

135

He looked at Colonel Primrose almost apologetically, as if only at long last getting to the point that had been raised.

"But the matter of evidence," he said. "And whether, if this had happened, you would have had a case. Let us suppose that I had done all this. I would sit probably where I sit now, and say to my friend who doesn't make many mistakes —and who I would be certain I could not deceive, 'If you have the legal evidence, admissible and incontrovertible in a court of law, to make me hang, I will hang with pleasure. Your duty is clear, and I know well that you have never failed it. You have no choice but to take your case to the public prosecutor. You have asked my opinion, and it is this. The public prosecutor is an honest man. He is also an able lawyer. He will ask for evidence before he brings this case to trial. As you know, a man may not be made to testify against himself. As a lawyer, I do not believe you have evidence enough to make him feel that he can present this case.' "

Horace Blodgett paused. When he spoke again his voice was clear and strong with profound conviction.

"But suppose, in such a case, that you or Bigges found evidence that enabled the prosecutor to bring me into court. I would have faith in a jury of twelve of my countrymen. And if they said, You may go, I would go . . . and if they said, You are convicted, and must hang by the neck until you are dead, I would accept that with only a natural and momentary regret. I would have no wish to subvert the law. I would stand, with a good heart, wherever it is to place me."

He looked steadily across his desk at Colonel Primrose.

I suppose I must have breathed, while he was talking, but I don't remember it. And Colonel Primrose certainly took a deep breath before he spoke.

"—Thank you, Horace," he said.

I don't ever remember seeing him so quietly urbane.

"I . . . had some idea that that's what you would tell me. I think your analysis included everything. And I suppose your opinion is right. My duty is clear, of course."

He was silent for a moment.

"It's unfortunate—or fortunate—that medical science is not able to say, accurately, when a man has died. And of course it's very much one or the other that Courtney broke up the record that was on Durbin's machine shortly after we got there. And under the circumstances it really is fortunate that no charge can be brought against either Duleep Singh or Sondauer. It actually was impossible for either of them to have done it."

Horace Blodgett nodded.

"No person may be placed in jeopardy of his life because of the act of another person. The moral law——"

He stopped and listened, that odd half-smile of his on his

face. I listened too, and heard the mild commotion at the front door that undoubtedly marked the return of the lady of the house. And in an instant Corinne sailed in, her hat awry, her face beaming.

"My dear Horace!—Oh, hello, Grace, my dear. Hello, John. I'm so glad to see you. My dears, do you know I've just met the most delightful man. He works in the Bureau of Engraving. It's simply fascinating. I was waiting for a bus, and he said, 'Lady, do you want a lift?' My dear, he brought me right to the corner. You see, Horace, it *is* the Power of Thought, because I've never hitch-hiked in my life before. The man was so nice. I can't tell you. Only, Horace, he said he didn't think the Power of Thought worked against people like the Nazis. He said he thought you had to . . . what word did he use?—implement it, with bombs, he said, and I dare say he's right. We really ought to know more people, Horace."

She flurried around, beaming and fussing with the odds and ends of books on the table. She settled down at last, and smiled at everybody.

And then a very strange thing happened.

"And now tell me what you've been doing," she said, and went straight on without waiting for anyone to answer. "John, you probably don't believe in the Power of Thought. But it works. I'm going to tell you something I've never told anybody, and I shall never speak of it again. It was the Power of Thought that killed Mr. Durbin. I know it's true, because from the day I first met him at Courtney's I've thought that he must die. And now that he's dead I shall try to find somebody to pray for him. Of course I couldn't possibly do it myself, but I dare say somebody will."

And then she actually said, "I'll give them my meat coupons, and I dare say they'll be glad to."

The look on Colonel Primrose's face I couldn't describe, and it was the first time, before or since, that I've ever seen Horace Blodgett look startled.

"Do you . . . did you know who Durbin was, Corinne?" he asked.

"Oh, of course, my dear!" she answered, so gently. "How could I forget him? I hoped you'd never know!"

And she added, quite in her own manner again, "But when you were so high and mighty about Courtney's marriage settlement, I knew you did. We'd have been in the poorhouse if you'd always been so particular."

She went over to him, bent down and kissed him. There were tears in her eyes, and I thought in Horace Blodgett's, but I wouldn't know.

"There, my dear," she said softly. "Now we must forget."

137

25

Colonel Primrose and I got in Sergeant Buck's car.

"What . . . will you do?" I asked.

He sat there silently for quite a little while. Then he looked around at me. "What will I do? Just what Horace said."

"You'll take it to the prosecutor?"

"Of course."

"Couldn't you just . . . hush and say nothing about it?" I asked hopefully.

He shook his head. "You and Buck again. What Horace said is not a legal confession and can never be used. I doubt if legally there's evidence enough to justify taking the case to trial. However, that's for the District Attorney to decide. If he does so decide, then it's up to Horace to say what his plea shall be, and finally it's up to a jury of his peers. All that lies beyond the point where the investigator has written 'Finis,' Mrs. Latham.

"It's an odd thing," he went on after a long pause. "In every murder I've investigated there's always been some unexpected circumstance no one could have foreseen reasonably. Fate always seems to step in. This is the only case I've been on where Fate favored the opposition. Normally it's the unexpected unforeseen thing that hangs a man. The reverse seems to be true here. No one could have known that it would be impossible for the coroner to say with any degree of accuracy at what time Durbin died. No one could have guessed that his last words, if he spoke any, were being recorded in the next room, or that they'd be destroyed by a woman thinking it was someone else she was saving. It almost looks as if this time Fate had taken a beneficent interest in shielding the agent she used to destroy a wicked man. And she seems to have done it pretty effectively. I have complete confidence that whatever is done, it will be done with honor. But it's out of my province. And I'm not a swami—I can't tell you what will happen."

"You can tell me how you knew," I said.

"He was the only person who could possibly have done it, as things developed," he said. "I knew Cass didn't. He might have gone in there and busted him on the jaw, and accidentally broken his neck. If he had he'd have gone to the nearest police station. He wouldn't have strangled him. But . . . I thought almost at the time it could have happened that way—when we were all there in the drawing room. Then it all sort of pieced together, after that. I knew about the Blodgett girl."

He didn't say anything for a minute.

"It was the anniversary of her death, of course. Then there were all sorts of other things. Horace's fury when Courtney wanted him to draw up her marriage contract with Durbin. That seemed to take some explanation. And at that dinner at their house Thursday night. I've never known him to serve champagne—and in the library, under the girl's picture. And you remember when we were talking about the pathological fear of cats. Horace began to say he'd known a young man who had it, and Corinne stopped him. Fear of cats isn't uncommon, but in a really morbid form you aren't likely to run into it personally twice in a lifetime. And Durbin had been here less than a year—this was the first anniversary of her death when he'd been around."

We'd passed Courtney's house. Even though Cass was probably still there it looked lonely and empty, I thought, rather like the big houses along Massachusetts Avenue before the war that used to be all boarded up, with agents' signs on them. The boards and the signs weren't there, but it seemed to me as if I could see their shadows already.

As we crossed the buffalo bridge to get to Georgetown he said, "I've invited a couple of people to your house this afternoon. I phoned while you and Corinne were upstairs. I hope you don't mind."

"No," I said. "Of course not. Who are they?"

"We'll see, if they turn up. I want you to meet Sondauer, if he hasn't gone to New York—or Brazil."

But it wasn't Mr. Sondauer, whom I still have to meet if he ever comes to Washington again. It was Molly and Cass. She'd got there already, when we went into the sitting room, and she and Sergeant Buck were out looking at the tomatoes. Just looking at him through the windows I could see that his opinion of me as a gardener was no higher than as anything else. Of course, I can't help it if the tomato worms drop out of a clear sky, and if he and Lilac both think my garden is funny who am I to say it isn't? I could hear him saying something about it, and Lilac's high-pitched cackle, as he went down to the kitchen when Molly came in.

"Hello!" she said. "Mr. Buck and I've been out to Walter Reed."

I began to see a strange light through all this. It seemed an odd way to entertain a young lady until you were ready for her, but I don't suppose Sergeant Buck ever goes to the movies. I looked at Colonel Primrose.

"I'm expecting Cass here, in a few minutes," he said.

"Cass? What . . . for?" Molly asked quickly. The pale glow that was in her cheeks as a result of an afternoon of good deeds with that lantern-jawed Boy Scout down in my

139

kitchen—and eating my ham, no doubt—faded instantly, and her eyes widened unhappily.

"Because I think that . . . well, that you two people are off on the wrong track, both of you."

The color flashed into her cheeks again. Her eyes darkened like smouldering coals.

"I wish you'd mind your own business, Colonel Primrose!" she said. "I know what I'm doing, and I don't need your— Oh, Grace, I can't, I tell you!"

The doorbell had rung, and he'd gone to answer it.

"I don't want to see him again, Grace—please!"

It was rather difficult, she was so shaken all of a sudden just at the sound of his voice. It didn't sound very reassuring to me as he said, "Well, here I am. I don't know what you want," to Colonel Primrose in the hall. It looked to me very much as if we were going to have a first-rate blow-up on our hands instead of anything else, and I was sure of it as I looked at Molly and saw her stiffening as if she'd been infected with a little of the congealing fluid that Sergeant Buck uses to try to hide his jelly-like interior. He's not a diamond in the rough, as I've heard him called—he's the custard center of a granite eclair. But while Molly looked like frozen marble her eyes were volcanic enough, and so were Cass's as he came in and saw her, and tightened up himself when the look in his eyes brought no response from hers.

There was certainly nothing in the atmosphere that could by any stretch of the imagination have led either of them to think the other cared a hang. I began to wonder whether I'd made up all the things they'd said to me, and I think even Colonel Primrose was a little discomfited. I looked at him anxiously.

He had his record book again, which Sergeant Buck must have brought over, and he took the top one out.

"This came off the D. J. Durbin production line a week ago Saturday," he said. "It was sorted away among those he apparently wasn't going to keep. It's rather interesting, though."

"I thought we were through with all that," Molly said quietly, and Cass said, "I don't like amateur performances, Colonel—would you mind playing something else?"

"I'm going to play this," Colonel Primrose said equably, "—and you two are going to listen to it, very carefully."

He put it on the turntable and switched the key. And again, as in the Crane-Armistead-Sondauer record we'd heard, I had the odd sensation of being moved instantly to another place, except that this wasn't just a room in a hotel but that very library where so much had happened.

At first there were just sounds of someone in a room, moving chairs and whistling softly. It was exactly like an overture at the theatre before the curtain rises. Then I heard Flowers' voice saying, "Oh, my laws." Then Courtney's voice and another, out of focus, and Courtney's voice then becoming quite clear.

"That's all right, Flowers—finish it later. Come on in, Dick. It's swell seeing you. I didn't know you were back. Let's go outside, it's cooler. How was Cass?"

How Molly, sitting beside me, could have stiffened any tighter I don't know, but she seemed to. I could feel it as she sat there bolt upright.

Then a man's voice.

"Sorry, I can't stay. I've got a car outside—have to get a plane for Dallas in half an hour. Cass is fine. He's coming home."

"Oh, how wonderful!"

"The point is, he doesn't know just when he gets in, and it's secret so he couldn't cable or write. He asked me to tell Molly he was coming. She isn't home and I don't know how to get in touch with her. So I thought you were their best friend and you'd tell her. I couldn't leave a note lying around. So tell her he's due in Wednesday or Thursday, and for her to call Two-two at the War Department and they'll tell her when the plane's landing. Will you do that, and keep it absolutely under your hat?"

And caught and preserved in that record was just the slight shade that came into Courtney Durbin's voice, as if she knew very well, at that moment, that she was never going to.

"Oh, of course, I'll be glad to."

"Well, I've got to shove. Be sure. Cass would kill me if I let him down. He's crazy about that gal, absolutely . . ."

The voice faded out, and the record ran on in silence, until I heard the closing of a door.

Molly sat by me perfectly still, hardly so much as breathing, and Cass stood there blankly, his cigarette burning almost to his fingers. Colonel Primrose switched off the record, without saying anything, and carefully closed the top of the phonograph.

"—Then . . . then you did want me to know?"

Molly's voice sounded very small, like a child's, and far away.

He looked at her, still speechless. Then he said, "Wasn't it you that . . . called up the War Department?"

141

"Why . . . no . . . I never knew, nobody ever told me,"
Molly said.

"Oh, honey!" he said then, and he was across the room,
and they were in each other's arms, half laughing and half
crying, both of them, and Cass saying, "Oh, gosh, Molly, I
love you so much!"

Colonel Primrose went over and carefully picked up the
cigarette Cass had dropped on the floor, and he and I went
out to look for some more tomato worms. But they look awfully like the leaves, and that's probably why I couldn't see
any. There were a lot of them there, apparently.

"What you need is some real nicotine," Colonel Primrose
said. "I'll give you the bottle that was in Durbin's desk drawer,
when the police get through with it, if you promise just to use
it out here.—Well, that's that," he went on. "I was afraid it
wasn't going to work, for a moment. I feel sorry for Cass. It's
a little hard for a man to tell a woman he loves her when he
doesn't get any encouragement."

He looked at me and smiled again.

"It must be," I said. "And one thing—I want to know why
Achille came to my door that night. Do you remember?"

He nodded. "Durbin wanted to make sure Molly was out of
the house. He knew Cass would kill him if anything happened
to her. There was one thing he was even more afraid of than
he was of cats, I think. And that was death. I've never seen a
gangster more safeguarded with warning devices."

"And the kitten?" I asked.

He looked around just to make sure.

"Horace's offices are in the building the pet shop's in."

He shrugged. "Armistead says Sondauer was never away
from him long enough to get to a pet shop, when he came
to think about it. Again, there is no proof."

We went back toward the house.

"And there's something I'd like to know," he said, "though
there isn't much doubt about it. We'll ask her."

They were still sitting hand in hand on the sofa when we
came in, and I've never seen two more radiant faces.

"We want to know something," Colonel Primrose said.
"What *were* you doing the night you were supposed to be in
bed here, when Achille was poisoned?"

Her eyes opened wider.

"I was going back home." Her hand tightened on Cass's.
"And I saw Randy bringing something out and Cass
opening the door of the shack on the corner. And the colored
woman across the street made me go in her house. She said
. . . she said the devil had just been there a little while before,
she'd seen him limping down the steps. She told me I mustn't
go in the house until the sun came up. I didn't really believe
it . . . but I thought if I did she wouldn't tell anybody. So I

came back here then. I . . . knew Randy and Cass hadn't . . . done anything, but I thought they'd be happier if they didn't know I'd been there. Did she—tell you?"

Colonel Primrose shook his head. "I just supposed you were there," he said. "I think your neighbors like you."

It was Lilac who said the final words, I think. Molly and Cass had gone home, and Sergeant Buck, and after supper Colonel Primrose went. Lilac came upstairs.

"Well," she said, "Mis' Courtney's got all the money she want—if that what she *does* want. But Miss Molly, she got Mr. Cass. They was over-rejoice, I reckon. Rejoicin' in *that* house tonight, I reckon. I jus' hope it stays rejoicin', but I 'spec' it will. Miss Molly's a nice chil'. She a *well-riz* chil'. An' Mr. Cass, he's a *nice* person."

Printed in Great Britain
by Amazon